AF445138

Cherokee Nation

Gabriel Murray

Cherokee Nation

Published by Pegasus Press

Contact; pegasusagent123@gmail.com

ISBN ; 9798671475104

John Ross (October 3, 1790 – August 1, 1866), "Mysterious Little White Bird"), was the Principal Chief of the Cherokee Nation from 1828–1866, serving longer in this position than any other person. Described as the Moses of his people, Ross influenced the Indian nation through such tumultuous events as the relocation to Indian Territory and the American Civil War. John Ross was the son of a Cherokee mother and a Scottish father. His mother and maternal grandmother were of mixed Scots-Cherokee ancestry, since his maternal grandfather was another Scottish immigrant. At the time among the matrilineal Cherokee, anyone born of a Cherokee mother was counted as a Cherokee, and a member of her clan.

The Trail of Tears

; was a series of forced relocations of approximately 60,000 Native Americans in the United States from their ancestral homelands in the South-eastern United States, to areas to the west of the Mississippi River that had been designated as Indian Territory. The forced relocations were carried out by government authorities following the passage of the Indian Removal Act in 1830. The relocated peoples suffered from exposure, disease, and starvation while en-route to their new designated reserve, and approximately 4,000 died before reaching their destinations or shortly after from disease. The forced removals included members of the Cherokee, Muscogee (Creek), Seminole, Chickasaw, and Choctaw nations, as well as their African slaves. The phrase "Trail of Tears" originates from a description of the removal of many Native American tribes, including the Cherokee Nation relocation in 1838. Between 1830 and 1850, the Chickasaw, Choctaw, Creek, Seminole, and Cherokee people (including mixed-race and black slaves who lived among them) were forcibly removed from their traditional lands in the South-eastern United States, and later relocated farther west. State and local militias forced Native Americans who were relocated to march to their destinations.[5] The Cherokee removal in 1838 (the last forced removal east of the Mississippi) was brought on by the discovery of gold near Dahlonega, Georgia in 1828, resulting in the Georgia Gold Rush. Approximately 2,000–8,000 of the 16,543 relocated Cherokee perished along the way.

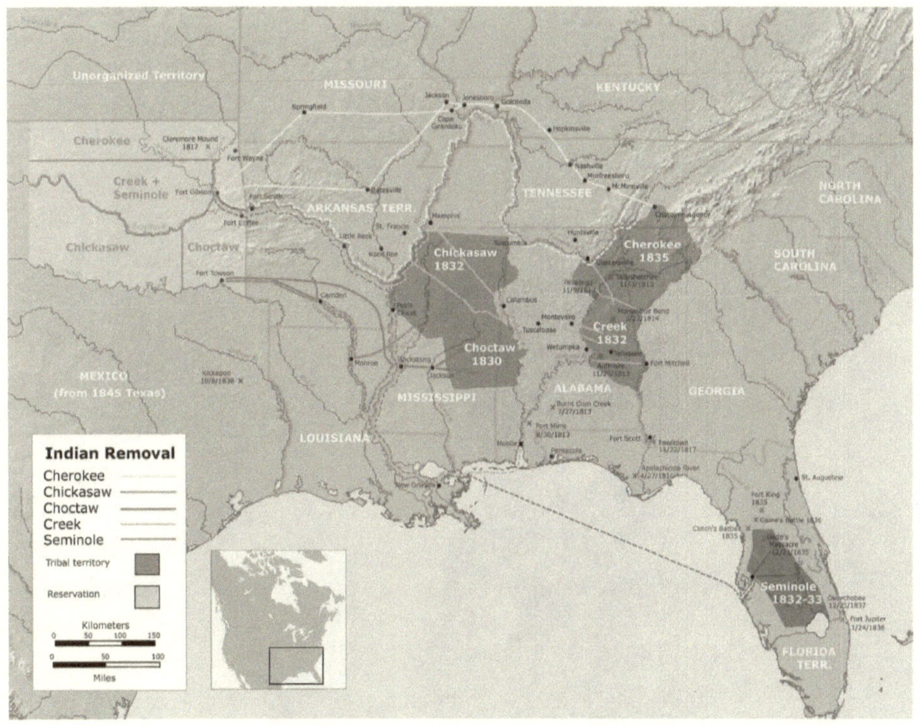

The story of Scotsman John Ross and his Cherokee friend Sequoyah, who tried to stop the American Government removal of the Cherokee Nation, from Georgia to Oklahoma. In May 1838, federal troops and state militia units, supervised by General Winfield Scott, rounded up the Cherokee, who refused to accept the Indian Removal Act, and forced them to make a one-thousand-mile journey across America, to a reservation in Oklahoma. This heroic journey is known as

'The Trail of Tears.

Sequoyah

1770-1843

Sequoyah (ᏍᏏᏆᏱ), as he signed his name, was a native of the Cherokee Nation. In 1821 he completed his independent creation of a Cherokee syllabary, making reading and writing in Cherokee possible. This was one of the very few times in recorded history that a member of a pre-literate people created an original, effective writing system). After seeing its worth, the people of the Cherokee Nation rapidly began to use his syllabary and officially adopted it in 1825. Their literacy rate quickly surpassed that of surrounding European-American settlers.

Cherokee Nation

The Story of the Trail of Tears

Gabriel Murray

Pegasus Press

PROLOGUE

The large grandfather clock was ticking, its pendulum swinging slowly and methodically. John Ross sat at a large oak desk. He was seventy eight years old now. His face was lined and furrowed, his hair and bushy eyebrows silvery grey and his hands gnarled and spotted. His eyes showed the wisdom and experience of a long adventurous life. A large bundle of letters and maps of America lay scattered on the desk. A small carving of an Indian warrior was placed by the ink well, and a miniature painting of an Indian woman. John Ross picked up the sharpened quill, dipped it in ink and began to write in his diary.

"It is thirty years since I took up the fight to preserve the nation of the Cherokee and their Eastern lands. I was born a Scotsman from Scot' settlers. I married a Cherokee woman named Quatie. I tried to protect her and her family, but in the end, I tried to save her and the Cherokee nation. This is the story of that struggle..."

He lay down the quill and opened the drawer. He lifted a necklace with a silver pendant of an eagle. He placed it on a large leather-bound book inscribed with the words 'Cherokee Nation'. John reflected back on his life. When he was young, the area around Rossville, Georgia was a vast open landscape of rivers, pine trees, rocks and waterfalls.

CHAPTER ONE

On a beautiful sunny spring day, the small Baptist Church of the Brainerd Mission by the Tennessee River, was packed to capacity. The Rev. Butrick played the wedding march on the piano to a large congregation full of Cherokee and white people.

John Ross and his Cherokee bride Quatie Henley Brown, both aged 21, stood in front of the minister, Rev. Butrick. John was dressed in long tight breeches, waistcoat and a white frilled shirt. Quatie wore full Indian dress with fringe and turquoise beads, a blue ribbon and white feathers bound into two long blue-black plaits. Quatie's family sat in the front pews among the white community. John Ross's father, Daniel Ross, and his wife Molly, were in attendance, dressed in their Sunday best. Sequoya, a 25-year-old Cherokee Indian with a long ponytail and beads around his neck, was watching the ceremony.

"We are gathered here today to join two people in the ceremony of marriage: John Ross and Quatie Brown. We welcome Quatie into this new Baptist church. We Baptists have come here, seeking refuge from persecution. We have been welcomed by the Cherokee. Many Indians have begun to worship here and we welcome them.

Under this new government of the United States, all men are equal, whatever race, colour or creed they belong to. So today I perform this mixed marriage, blessed by God. Will you, John Ross, take this Cherokee woman, Quatie Henley Brown to be your lawfully wedded wife."

***

Sequoyah was busy in his workshop, working away on some silver, when John Ross entered. The Cherokee looked up.

"I was looking for you," said John. "Can you make something for Quatie?"

"Yes," Sequoyah agreed, "I can make her a beautiful Cherokee necklace." John discovered some parchment on the table.

"What's this?" he asked. Sequoyah stopped working and poured over the parchments.

"It's called talking leaves," he explained, "the language of the Cherokee. I am trying to create letters for the Cherokee language, create a character for each word, each word is divided, to create one character for each letter."

John smiled: "If you have cracked the Cherokee language, we white can speak directly with the Indians. Sequoyah, this is important work, very important." He paused, remembering something. There was another reason he had come into Sequoyah's workshop, besides getting a present for his bride.

"You must come with me to meet Elias," he continued. "He has set up a printing press, to print a new newspaper for the Cherokee." 2.

John Ross and Sequoyah rode to the printing office of the Cherokee Phoenix. They tied up their horses and entered the small single-story building, mainly made from wood. They walked past men working at printing presses, into Elias Boudinot's office at the back. Elias was delighted to see them and welcomed them both.

"Mr. Ross, thank you for coming." The men shook hands.

"I discovered that Sequoyah has been working on a Cherokee, English alphabet." said John.

"Let me see." Elias showed great interest. He was a small built, slender man with unruly dark hair and large, lively dark eyes. John took out Sequoyah's parchments and spread them on the desk. Elias studied the parchments carefully.

"Yes," he said. "It is a clear translation; we could use it. Sequoyah, this is a work of genius. Do you know what this means? All Cherokee can now speak with the world."

"Thank you," Sequoyah acknowledged. "I have been working on it for many years." Elias continued with excitement in his voice:

"We can publish the first translation of the bible, into Cherokee language."

"Extraordinary work." John nodded.

"John," Elias suggested. "I would like you to write an article for the Cherokee Phoenix to comment on Indian affairs. It will be read in Washington, where it matters." John Ross agreed and said he would be pleased to.

"There are 18,000 Indians in the Cherokee Nation," said Elias, "we must fight to protect them."

CHAPTER TWO

John Ross had so many flashbacks at once. At 78, he felt he needed to write everything down as he remembered it. He sat there at the desk with quill in hand, thinking of a peaceful time, when he, Quatie and their three children, were all together in their house in Rossville, Georgia. His mind tried to hold on to the picture of his children playing. James was five, Jane three, and Allen just two years old.

He continued to write:

"I and my wife Quatie lived in peace, for many years and had three beautiful children. Our children that were half Indian and half white. They belonged to a new rainbow nation of mixed peoples. I believed that America was changing, adapting to its new immigrants." He remembered the Indian postman riding up on horseback delivering a letter to his house.

"One day a letter arrived from Washington, that changed the course of my life and the fate of the whole Cherokee Nation forever."

In January 1814 the Creek Indians of northern Alabama and Georgia attacked white settlements. Four hundred settlers were killed, at the Fort Mims Massacre by Creek Indians. President Madison sent for General Andrew Jackson to come to the White House to discuss how to deal with this serious matter.

"Mr. President, I came as soon as I received your message." said General Jackson. President Madison looked at a map of America, and asked Jackson to take a seat. The President told him:

"I want you, General Jackson, to take your men and sort this out."

"What do you want to do, Mr. President?"

"My plan is to move these Indians east." continued President Madison. "But I want you first to arrest the leaders of this massacre and bring them to trial, in a military court and if found guilty, execute them."

"The Indians have many guns, Mr. President, it will not be easy."

"We will have to make an example of them," the President insisted. "White folk must be protected."

"Yes, Mr. President, I will carry out your orders immediately." said Jackson. "But first can I try and negotiate with the Creek leaders, for a surrender. I know one man that may help us. He has been writing on Indian affairs."

"Who is that?" The President frowned.

"A man named John Ross," Jackson told him. "I am told that he is married to a Cherokee woman in Georgia. He knows all of the Indian leaders."

"You can talk with him," the President shrugged, "but I need you to call in the militias in the area. Some, I believe, are made up of Cherokees. They are traditional enemies of the Creek, so they can be persuaded to fight with us."

***

John Ross paced up and down the grounds of the Baptist church, thinking, trying to come up with a solution. The Rev. Butrick and the Rev. Bushyhead could see that something was troubling him.

"What is the problem, John?" asked Rev. Bushyhead. John took a letter out of his pocket and handed it to him.

"It arrived from General Jackson from Washington today." said John. "The Creek have killed white settlers. He wants me to go and negotiate with the Creek leaders, for a surrender. If not the Creek leaders will be arrested and face execution."

"The Creek lands are being invaded by white settlers." Bushyhead commented in a sad voice.

"Why are we going to get sucked into this war." Rev. Butrick joined the conversation. John was seriously concerned now.

"How long will it be before Cherokee lands are taken."

"I am worried about this, too." said Bushyhead. "Surely under our constitution, Indian rights will be respected."

"I can see dark times ahead." said John. Rev. Bushyhead was in full support of him.

"We are building schools for the Indians, this is not a time for war."

"I do not want to go on this trip," John sighed. "But if I can help save the Creek, I will go." John had sent for Sequoyah, who arrived on horseback. He had received a message, but was so far unaware why John Ross was looking for him.

"I have news from Washington." John explained. "I have been asked by General Jackson to negotiate a surrender of the Creek Indians, they have killed white settlers, in Alabama."

Sequoyah shook his head.

"The Creek will not surrender; they are a proud people."

"I want you to ride with me, you know the Indian trails."

"You must be good to your mother, when I am gone." John Ross had said to his children, when they ran to him.

(Check dates! If they got married in 1812, they would not have had 3 children in 1814.)

"I'll miss you," said Quatie.

"Dont worry I will not be gone for long." He assured his wife.

After he had said a long and emotional 'good bye' to Quatie and the children, John Ross and Sequoyah made their way on horseback to John's father's house in Rossville, Georgia.   His parents stood in the porch waiting for them. Daniel Ross wore a long-tailed coat, a plain shirt and breeches. Molly Ross was dressed in a plain blue, high-waisted dress, and a brown shawl around her shoulders. Her dark hair was pinned up under a brown felt bonnet. John dismounted and hugged his mother, then his father. They did not smile.

"Look after yourself, son." said Molly, with a tear in

her eye.

"Son," said Daniel, "we are from good Scots roots. We escaped Scotland to find peace and freedom after the English took our lands. Now we are being forced into some land war. Before long this whole problem will be on our doorstep."

"Your right," John sighed. "We are being drawn into this. We white folk live peacefully among the Cherokee."

"Don't forget," his mother reminded him, "you have Cherokee blood in your veins, your grandmother was Cherokee."

CHAPTER THREE

So, John mounted his horse and set out with Sequoyah. They crossed the mountain trail and rode along wild, rocky paths, with Sequoyah guiding John through the Creek Nation territory. They found no signs of any other riders having been on this path recently, until they reached the American Army Camp. Tents of various sizes were arranged in regimented rows.

A soldier in uniform stood watch and greeted them with some suspicion, as they rode down the hill.

"I am looking for General Jackson." said John.

"Who might you be?" The soldier wanted to know. John handed him the letter from General Jackson.

"Ok, follow me."

They dismounted and tied up their horses outside General Jackson's tent. Inside, the General was looking at maps, spread across a table, when John and Sequoyah entered.

"John Ross at your service, sir."

"Mr. Ross, thank you for coming." Jackson looked up. "Who is this with you.?" John introduced his friend:

"This is Sequoyah, he is Cherokee."

Jackson nodded in acknowledgement. Then turned to John:

"You received my letter."

"Yes, Sir." said John. The General spoke to him:

"I understand that you are married to an Indian and you know the tribal leaders."

"That is true, sir."

"You know the situation, the Creek have attacked and killed white settlers." John was defensive:

"Yes, but they stole their lands."

"I will give the Creek one last chance." said Jackson. "The Creek are in Horseshoe Bend, Alabama. I want you to visit the Creek leaders and get them to surrender." 4.

Sequoyah and John rested for a while and allowed the horses to feed and rest, before riding on into Creek Valley, Alabama. They crossed through rocky hillside and fertile prairie, where buffalo grazed and eagles flew above. It was a raw, but peaceful land, until they approached the Creek camp, that was guarded by Indians with guns and rifles. They all wore war paint and were ready to defend themselves and their land, if needed. Sequoyah made a sign of peace. He and John dismounted their horses. Two painted, bare-chested warriors took them to a campfire. Here they were greeted by Selocta, Chief of the Creek and his war council of five old Indians, all in full war dress and paint.

"What brings you here, John Ross?" asked the Chief.

"This is Sequoyah, my guide." John introduced his companion. "He is Cherokee."

"We are not friends of the Cherokee." said Selocta. "Why have you come?"

"General Jackson has asked me to come, to get you to surrender."

Chief Selocta remained defensive.

"The Creek never surrender. The white man has taken our lands to the west, some of our braves attacked them. They were only defending what is theirs."

"Yes, but you have killed white men. You have one last chance, surrender and you will live. If you don't, you will all die. How many of your tribes' people are here?"

"One thousand Creek Warriors and three hundred fifty women and children." The Chief knew the exact number. "Last century an old wise woman of the Creek Indian nation, named 'Eyes of Fire', had a vision of the future. She prophesied that one day, because of the white man's greed, there would come a time, when the earth would be ravaged and polluted, the forests destroyed, the birds would fall from the air, the waters would be blackened, the fish being poisoned in the streams, and the trees destroyed, mankind will cease to exist. Tell your general we will fight to the end, there will be no surrender."

***

John Ross returned to General Andrew Jackson's Command Post, with a heavy heart.

"So, what did they have to say?" asked the General in a tone of voice that suggested he already knew the answer.

"No surrender, sir." said John.

"Then we will capture them and execute the guilty ones."

"We can surround them and wait them out, Sir." John still tried to negotiate. Jackson rolled his eyes at John showing his unwillingness to compromise.

"No. We don't have time for that."

"You cannot kill innocent women and children." insisted John. General Jackson raised his voice.

***

In March 27, 1814 in Creek Valley Alabama, one thousand American soldiers stood ready to attack a barricaded bunker, defended by one thousand Creek warriors. They were supported by two hundred Cherokee Indians. Americans began their attack. The Creek returned their gunfire, pinning the U.S. soldiers down. Heavy cannons boomed as the U.S. artillery bombed the Creek fortress.

John and Sequoyah watched the battle. In the distance, a hundred Creek warriors fought at the barricades. Some Creek women and children were killed. Some children were left to wander alone among their dead parents, covered in blood.

On the battlefield at Horseshoe Bend the American army charged up the hill. Creek warriors lined up and returned the gunfire. A hundred more Creeks attack them with knives and hatchets. An arrow hit General Jackson in the shoulder. Sequoyah rushed forward and saved the General. (How? What did he do?)

Chief Selocta and his war council were captured. (Describe how)

General Jackson was carried to an army tent by some of his soldiers. A Doctor pulled the arrow from his shoulder and bandaged his upper arm. John and Sequoyah watched.

"Don't worry, you will survive." The Doctor told the General.

***

In the Creek war camp, General Jackson was sitting with Chief Selocta and his war council; surrounded by soldiers pointing their rifles at them. General Jackson looked at a large map of Creek territory. He had drawn up a contract and signed it.

"For your crime," the General spoke directly to the Creek Chief, "the Creek Nation must give us 22,000,000 acres." Jackson placed the contract on the table and handed Selocta an ink quill. He pointed at a place under his own signature, and commanded:

"Sign h6.

The Governor of Georgia lived in and worked from a great stately house. Governor Troup stood at the entrance to the building with some officials. They had not expected General Jackson and his troops just yet, and were surprised to see them riding up the main street so soon.

"The war is over," Jackson announced. "We have made a deal with the Creek."

CHAPTER FOUR

"Good to see you General." said Governor Troup and introduced the man standing to the right of him. "This is my secretary, Mr. Andrew Lumkin."

Troup and his officials invited General Jackson to the Governor's office inside the house. The Governor sat down at his desk and asked Jackson to take a seat.

"So, what deal did you make with the Creek?" asked Troup.

"22,000,000 acres," replied Jackson.

"That's a mighty lot of land." acknowledged the Governor.

"Yes," continued Jackson, "but now, we need to move the Cherokee west of the Mississsppi."

"I agree," Troup nodded. "I want to remove the Cherokee."

"We have done it with the Creek," said Jackson, "we can certainly remove the Cherokee."

Governor Troup sat back in his chair.

"You're right, we have too many emigrants arriving. God fearing folk. We need more land. Why not set up a lottery and give land to any able-bodied man, that can defend it."

"The Cherokee believe that they have a Cherokee Nation."

"What nation?" The Governor frowned. "They live in the united states of America. The land is just as much their's as ours."

"Then we will pay them for it a few dollars an acre." Jackson suggested. Troup was not convinced.

"They have millions of acres."

"There are 18,000 Cherokee, they will be given land to the east."

"There are thousands of settlers arriving every day." Troup did not want to compromise.

"I am going back to Washington," said Jackson. "I will talk to President Madison. I d'ont believe that these Indians belong here anymore. Some of them have become Christian's. But they don't belong among white men. They will be given their own reservations."

Governor Troup was pleased with what he heard.

"I will appoint Mr. Lumkin to organise a land lottery of Cherokee lands."

"There is gold in Cherokee lands." Andrew Lumkin spoke up. "We have thousands of immigrants on the way. We need to divide the Indian lands into plots."

"What price would you suggest?" asked Troup.

"Forty acres sell for 40$." said Lumkin. "One dollar an acre!" Governor Troup smiled. He liked that idea.

"The state of Georgia and the banking system could make millions of dollars from that sale. What we need to do is force the Cherokee out of the eastern lands."

General Jackson knew that was not going to be easy.

"It may be difficult. The Cherokee Indians are building schools and churches, they are no longer the primitive folk, you think they are. Many have become Christians."

"Look," Governor Troup insisted. "We can force Washington to move the Indians out of these lands. Divide and conquer. Find Indians among them that can be bribed, we can offer them money and land to the west."

"Where do you suggest?"

"Oklahoma." The Governor seemed to have it all worked out. "Look, General Jackson, we don't want no Indians around here. If you assist us, you will get well rewarded. Have you any ambitions, General Jackson?"

"Yes," Jackson straightened himself. "I am entering political life and will try for election. Maybe I will be president one day." The Governor was impressed with the General's pride and ambition.

"Let me promise you, if you assist the state of Georgia, I will make sure that my friends in Washington look after you. I am a Freemason; I will make you a member. You sort these indians out for me, and I will make sure you become the next President of the United States."

General Jackson was well pleased with his prospects. 7.

Quatie looked out of the window of her home in Rossville, Georgia and smiled, as she saw her husband John and his friend Sequoyah approaching on horseback. The children ran out to greet their father.

John's parents came out into the porch.

"We worried about you!" said his father with genuine concern.

"We prayed for you!" said his mother.

John and Sequoyah entered the house and gratefully eat some hot food.

"What happened to the Creek?" enquired Daniel Ross.

"They lost everything, 22,000,000 acres of land." said John. His father looked shocked.

"But that must be all of Creek lands!"

"Yes," John told him, "and American troops have murdered hundreds of innocent women and children at the battle of Horseshoe Bend and hung its leaders."

"The whites do not want the Indians in eastern lands

any more!" Daniel Ross sighed.

"What about Cherokee lands?

''They will take our land, too."

***

One afternoon on Ross Farm, John saw an old Indian riding towards him. He wore traditional Indian dress – fringed suede tunic and trousers. His long thick grey hair tied back into a ponytail and around his neck an impressive silver and turquoise beaded necklace with three small blue feathers. His outfit proved to John that he must be a man of authority. The Indian dismounted and introduced himself.

"My name is Chief Pathkiller, Chief of the Cherokee."

"Pleased to meet you." said John. The Indian Chief continued:

"They told me you married Quatie, a Cherokee girl. I came to welcome you into our Cherokee Nation."

"Thank you, Sir." said John.

"They tell me that you were at the battle of the Creek Indians."

"It was a massacre!"

"I want to talk to you about the Cherokee." said Chief Pathkiller.

"How can I help you.?" John wondered.

"I need a white man to help me fight Washington and represent the Cherokee nation. They do not trust the Indians, but a Christian white man they will." John considered this for a moment.

"But my life is here in Georgia, not Washington!" he exclaimed. Chief Pathkiller remained calm.

"I understand, but the white man intrudes on our land and we need your help. You are the one who can help us; you are an educated man, they will respect you."

John Ross was taken by surprise.

Does the Cherokee council want this?"

"Yes," said the Chief of the Cherokee, "that is why I came."

"I'll go and meet them." John agreed.

Chief Pathkiller got on his horse and noticed Negro farm workers. He frowned.

"Why do you keep slaves?"

"They belong to my father." John told him. "I am hoping the government will grant them freedom. Some I have helped escape north."

Chief Pathkiller turned and rode away.

***

CHAPTER FIVE

John returned home and had to tell his wife yet again that he was leaving for a few days.

"The Cherokee council want to meet me."

"Do you know why?" asked Quatie. John told her about his encounter with Chief Pathkiller. Then continued: 8.

John Ross and Sequoyah travelled across the mountains, along the trail to the Cherokee Woods.

In the Long House a council of nineteen Cherokee men attended a meeting. Chief Pathkiller sat at the council table with Charles Hicks, a Cherokee with thick gray hair. Chief Pathkiller welcomed John and Sequoyah. Then he introduced them to the other council members. Elijah Hicks, Hair Conrad, Daniel Colton, Rev. Jesse Bushyhead, Rev. S. Foreman, Choowalooka, Moses Daniel, James Brown, Charles Hicks, George Hicks, John Drew, Richard Taylor, Peter Hilderbrand, John Ridge and Elias Boudinot.

"Gentlemen," said Chief Pathkiller, "this is John Ross."

"I am pleased to meet you all." said John. They all lifted their hands in greeting. Chief Pathkiller turned toward everyone.

"Charles Hicks has some news from Washington."

"I have received news from Washington," Charles Hicks told them, "that they have sworn in General Jackson as President."

"We all know that Jackson is no friend of ours." said John Ross. "I have also had news today, that gold has been discovered in Georgia. Thousands of immigrants are on their way to take Cherokee lands in North Georgia. Govenor George Tuft is organizing a lottery distributing Cherokee lands among the white. This is criminal, Georgia has no right to enter Cherokee lands. President Jackson is a friend of the Governor of Georgia. We will have to take this case to the highest office."

"But we will not get much sympathy from the President." said Chief Pathkiller.

"There must be some justice in Washington." John was hopeful.

The Georgians have a history of stealing land." continued Charles Hicks. "Corrupt officials made grants of millions of acres that did not exist over thirty years ago. Then the land was sold to speculators."

"Yes," John Ross nodded. "I remember that land scam – The Yazoo Fraud. The government had to pay for this fraud, with $4.3 million dollars." Pathkiller's eyes flashed with anger.

"Stealing Indian lands and selling land that does not exist!"

Charles Hicks was also enraged:

"Who are these men? Do they not have any God!"

John Ross had wondered about this, too.

"The Cherokees have begun to abandon hunting and their traditional ways of life and instead learn how to live, worship, and farm like Christians. Many Cherokees embrace the new religion of the white man. They have built churches. White people in Georgia and other southern states that are on the borders of the Cherokee Nation, refuse to accept the Cherokee people as social equals and have urged their political representatives to seize the Cherokee land."

"But we will not get much sympathy from the President." said Chief Pathkiller.

"After the purchase of the Louisiana Territory from France in 1803, U.S. President Thomas Jefferson wanted to relocate the eastern tribes beyond the Mississippi River."

"Jefferson did not believe in forceful removal." said John Ross. "We are heading into to dangerous waters. I will travel to Washington and get the government to stop Georgians invading our lands. Sequoyah will come with me. I will go and see the Secretary of War."

"John," Charles Hicks addressed him directly. "We want to nominate you, to be Chosen Chief of the Cherokee Nation."

"Chosen Chief!" John was a little surprised.

"Yes," confirmed Charles Hicks, "the Cherokee people need you." John Ross felt honoured as well as perplexed.

"What makes you think they will listen to me. I am only twenty-six years old." (Check what year is this now? He was 21 in 1812.)

"We will lose all Cherokee lands," said Charles Hicks, "like the Creek lost theirs, if we do not fight the government."

"I have a family here," John continued. "I have no time to go to Washington, it's over a thousand miles away." (? - Just a minute ago he said he was going)

"We need you John." urged Chief Pathkiller. "Look at the Creek, they have lost all their lands. If we do not go to Washington, there will be nothing left of the Cherokee nation. Your wife's family will lose everything. We need you in Congress to fight our cause. The clock is ticking, we have little time left. The Cherokee Council will pass a series of laws creating a national government, we want you to lead them. What do you say, John?"

Quatie was pleased to see her husband return home safe and in good health. However, John did not look happy.

"Tell me what happened." She said later that night, when the children were asleep.

"The governor of Georgia has started a lottery for Cherokee lands. I may have to go to Washington and try and stop him."

"They took the Creek lands," Quatie said scornfully, "now it's the Cherokee!"

John told her everything that had come to pass. Then Sequoyah arrived.

"Better get dressed." He said with alarm. "Chief Pathkiller's very ill."

"What has happened?" John demanded to know. The Chief of the Cherokee was very old.

John and Sequoyah quickly made their way to the chamber (or tent?) where Pathkiller lay dying. John placed his hand on his. The old man struggled to speak:

"John, thank you for coming. My friend, when I go. Please try and save the Cherokee Nation."

John knelt at Pathkiller's side. The old Cherokee Chief continued:

"The Great Spirit gave us this country as our home and to live on, and buffalo, deer and antelope. But the white man has come here, taking our land and killing our buffalo. They say that we are not civilized? We must continue to live as our fathers did, and their fathers before them. I must go, the great spirit is calling me. The destiny of our people's in your hands. May the great spirit bless you in the task ahead." Pathkiller gripped John's arm and then let go. He then breathed his last breath.

***

Many Cherokee gathered around a funeral pire. A Medicine Man, in traditional Cherokee dress and full headdress with large impressive eagle feathers, spoke some noble words in the Cherokee language, then and lit up the pire. The flames began to engulf Chief Pathkiller's body.

At night Charles Hicks and Sequoyah visited John Ross in his home. John asked if there was any news.

"I learnt today," said Charles Hicks, "that the governor of Georgia plans on enacting a law which strips the Cherokee of their land rights and remove them to the East."

"I must go to Washington immediately." John decided.

"Sequoyah will you come with me. You know the trails."

"Of course, but it's over a thousand miles over

mountains and great valleys."

"That's what they are hoping in Washington," said John, "that no Cherokee will come to stop their great plan."

Once again John had to say goodbye to Quatie, his children and his parents. He mounted his horse and rode away with Sequoyah.

They rode across the vast open countryside of prairie, rocks and woodland, along winding rocky paths and through fords of rivers. They stopped at night, to rest themselves and their horses, to find food and refresh themselves. They met no-one along the way. They crossed Georgia, South Carolina, North Carolina and Virginia, through great valleys and mountain passes.

They looked towards the capital and saw the outline of the great American city. They rested once more before riding into Washington.

***

CHAPTER SIX

Sequoyah and John entered the Meeting Room in the White House. The U.S. Commissioner to the Cherokee, Rev. John Schermerhorn, and the Secretary of War, John C. Calhoun were already seated, awaiting them.

"Gentlemen," Schermerhorn addressed them, "thank you for coming."

"Gentlemen, John C., Calhoun, Secretary of War." Calhoun introduced himself. "What can I do for you?" His appearance did not match his character. While his manner was austere and his voice without passion, he had a look of a wild man about him that not many would want to challenge. Grey piercing eyes flashed like daggers and a mean straight mouth in a furrowed face framed by a thick grey mane of unruly hair.

"Georgians are invading Cherokee lands." John Ross went straight to the point. "We want the government to stop this!"

Calhoun showed an expression of total indifference in his voice:

"The President informs me, that he is drawing up a treaty for the Cherokee, to offer you land and dollars to move east."

"You have already taken the lands of the Creek." said John. Calhoun continued:

"President Jackson believes that the solution to the Indian problem, is removal to the east. He does not believe in integration of Indians with the whites!"

John felt anger rising within him, but remained composed, as he spoke:

"The Cherokee are just as civilized as the whites. Some of them have become Chrisitans and have built churches and schools."

"Gentlemen," said Calhoun, "the President fought in the Indians wars, like you, Mr. Ross. He has had first-hand experience of the Indians, that is his solution."

John was rather annoyed with the Secretary of War, who seemed to have no mind or opinion of his own, but copied every word and idea of the President as absolute law.

"The only thing to do, is to sue Governor Tuft." John suggested. Calhoun shrugged:

"If you feel you have a case, sue him. He's the man responsible. President Jackson has been considering signing an Indian Removal Act."

"An Act," John could no longer hide his anger in his voice. "You want to legalise Georgia's illegal claims. We will have to petition the Congress!" 11.

In January 1829 John Ross and Sequoyah consulted John H. Eaton in his office in Washington.

"Thank you for seeing me, sir." said John. "This is Sequoyah, my Cherokee guide."

"Mr. Calhoun informed me that you were in Washington." Eaton started the conversation. "I spoke to the President this morning. I am sorry to tell you that President Jackson will support the right of Georgia to extend her laws over the Cherokee Nation."

"Can I petition Congress?" asked John.

"That is a good idea." Eaton seemed certainly more approachable than Calhoun. "I will help you with the application."

Eaton took two envelopes from his desk drawer and opened them.

"There are two other men that have come here to oppose the Indian Removal Act."

"Who are they?" John Ross was surprised.

"Let me see," said Eaton, perusing the letters. "Davy Crockett and Jeremiah Evarts, a Christian missionary. I will introduce you to them, come with me."

"I have heard of Davy Crockett," said John, "the great frontiers man."

***

John and Sequoyah followed John H. Eaton to the Congress Saloon, where Davy Crockett was engaged in conversation with Jeremiah Everts. Davy Crockett was dressed in frontier clothes, to some part Indian in style and a striking 'ten large gallon' hat. (Would he have worn a hat indoors?) Evarts, in contrast wore a fairly plain suit with a cravat around his neck.

"Let me introduce you to Mr. Davy Crockett and Mr. Jeremiah Evarts." said Eaton. "This is John Ross, chosen Chief of the Cherokee Nation, and his guide Sequoyah." Davy Crockett turned towards them.

"We have come to support you. We have heard of your cause. Gentlemen, you all know me as a frontiers man and now as a member of Congress. I have come here today to oppose the Indian Removal Act."

"I travelled in the south," said Jeremiah Everts, "and met the various tribes, I have seen integration with the white population. You have called the Cherokee the five civilized tribes. Yet they now want them removed."

"God will protect the Cherokee!" John Ross called out with passion. "This Act is not only unjust but un-Christian. If any of the Congress members have any goodness left in their hearts, they should vote against this act!"

***

The Congress Hall was filled with congressmen. When President Jackson arrived, the Congress stood to attention. He took a seat and the Congress sat also. Governor Troup also appeared. A Speaker got up and announced:

"In response to a petition made by Mr. John Ross, leader of the Cherokee Nation. I open the argument on the Indian Removal Act to the floor."

John Ross got up and looked across the Congress Hall at all the Senators.

"For thousands of years," he began, "the Cherokee tribes have lived in peace on the east coast of America. Now, because of Georgia's greed for gold and land, this nation that has its own government and in effect its own state, is being dissolved. Tell me, what legal right does Georgia have over Indian lands? This Indian Removal Act is unjust and every civilized man here should oppose it. It seems clear to me, that this removal act is an act to steal land and gold from our Indian nation. Georgia and Governor Troup has demanded these land rights. Now we have been forced into a situation of approving this treaty, that has no approval of the Cherokee Nation."

"We will now take a vote on this act." said the Speaker.

"231 votes for, 2 against." said the Speaker. "This Congress has endorsed President Jackson's policy of removal of Indians to the East by passing the Indian Removal Act, which allows the president to set aside lands west of the

Mississippi in exchange for the lands of the Indian nations in the east." Davy Crockett was furious:

"This is a barbaric Act and a selfish land grab by the American Government. There is no justice in this. The Cherokee Nation will fight for its rights. This is an unjust act. Our founding fathers believed in freedom and the rights of man. Surely in this land the new land of the United States, that other states cannot steal land from each other. In protest, I am resigning from this congress. You are all involved in this legalized crookery."

John looked around and observed a deaf silence among the Congress members.

***

A meeting was held in the Corridor of Congress Hall. John H. Eaton introduced John Ross to Senator Webster and Senator Frelinghuysen, a lawyer. Also present were Davy Crockett, Jeremiah Everts and William Wirt.

"It's final, Mr. Ross," said Eaton, "Congress has rejected your plea." If he spoke with regret, it had no bearing on the decisive outcome of the vote.

"I will not give up," John was determined. "I will take this all the way to the high court. There must be some justice! Thank you for your support, Mr. Crockett, you did not have to resign!" Davy Crockett shook his head:

"I cannot support this white run government anymore."

"God will judge them!" said Jeremiah Evarts, convinced of divine justice. William Wirt had listened in silence until now. Finally, he spoke:

"I am a lawyer, I will help you defend Cherokee rights, before the U.S. Supreme Court."

"Thank you for your support, gentlemen." said John.

***

Sequoyah and John Ross attended the Supreme Court with John Wirt. Chief Justice John Marshall read:

"In response to the case brought by Chief John Ross of the Cherokee Indians, cited as Cherokee Nation v. Georgia and Worcester v. Georgia. The United States of America does not, or never acknowledged that the Cherokee were a sovereign nation. We cannot defend the Cherokee from Georgia's laws. The Cherokee Nation

claim is denied on the grounds that the Cherokees are a 'domestic dependent sovereignty' and as such do not have the right to sue Georgia as a nation state." He cleared his throat and continued:

"The Cherokee are considered sovereign enough to legally resist the government of Georgia, and were encouraged to do so. However, the Cherokee are ultimately dependent on the federal government and are not a true nation state, nor fully sovereign."

John H. Eaton talked to John Ross, Sequoyah and John Wirt, outside his office.

"Mr. Ross, I regret to inform you that Mr. John Ridge is in Washington at this very moment talking to President Jackson about a treaty to hand over Cherokee lands. He has called his delegation the Ridge Party."

John Ross was utterly shocked.

"I cannot believe that he would betray us."

***

In May 1832 John Ridge and Elias Boudinot talked privately about the situation, with Supreme Court Justice John McClean.

"I am losing faith in John Ross." complained John Ridge. "If we are not careful, we will have no lands east or west."

"Then take the reservation to the east," said McClean, "and appoint a delegate in Congress."

"That way we could vote John Ross out of power." said Ridge.

***

A receptionist handed a letter to John Ridge at his hotel. He opened it immediately and read:

"Request urgent meeting. John Ross."

So, John Ross and Sequoyah met with Elias Boudinot and John Ridge at the Capitol Hotel in Washington, and questioned their decision.

"Yes, it is true," said Ridge, "I and Elias had a meeting with the chief court justice John McClean, we agreed with him that we can no longer support your plan to save the Cherokee Nation."

"If we all do not stand together against Washington, they will destroy us." John Ross was dismayed.

"We have no rights," said Elias, "can you not see, Indian lands belong to the United States. The governor of Georgia is pressing for removal of all Indians. Some Indians may live in peace, but some of the tribes kill whites, there is fear among them."

"We can all live in peace, whatever the colour of their skin." John Ross was convinced. Elias shook his head:

"Washington does not see it that way, especially President Jackson. He wants to rid all eastern lands of this problem."

"Do we not have rights?" John raised his voice. "Have the Indians not lived here for thousands of years!"

"We belong to the United States now," Ridge seemed to claim defeat, "the final decision comes from Washington."

"There must be a compromise," John Ross insisted, "where Indians can live with whites." He could not understand why Ridge and Boudinot, being of Cherokee origin themselves, could want to betray their own people.

"We disagree," said Ridge, "we resign from this council, along with others that will come with us."

John Ross looked each of them in the eye, as if searching for some answer that way.

"Do you realise what this means," he said. "It is over a thousand miles to the

western states. Your plan means up-rooting women, children, old people, and forcing them to march across the American wilderness. It would be genocide; thousands will die of exposure and exhaustion!"

John Ridge and Elias Boudinot stood up and walked out silently. John Ross turned to Sequoyah:

"I want you to get signatures from every Cherokee. This list you will bring to Washington, it will be a petition to the president."

"It will take time." said Sequoyah.

"Make haste, Sequoyah," urged John. "It is the last hope for the Cherokee Nation." 13.

One month later, at John Ross's home in Georgia, Sequoyah brought a giant heavy leather-bound folder and placed it on John's desk. It was bound with leather string and 300 pages long. Sequoyah was very pleased with this.

"Here it is," he said, "15,423 signatures."

"That's ninety percent of the Cherokee Nation." John took this as great news.

He opened the folder and looked at the long line of names.

"It's like the first Cherokee census," he said, "it will be helpful, if we have to organise a move west."

***

John and Sequoyah made another long journey to Washington, to present the petition to President Jackson.

The President was writing at his desk when John Ross entered. He looked up and admitted:

"It's been a long time since we met."

"Mr. President," replied John, "thank you for seeing me."

"It's a very serious matter," said the President, "but we need to resolve it. I saw Mr. Ridge and Mr. Boudinot the other day. I can see that there is a split on policy in the Cherokee Nation. I have here a treaty, that they have agreed to sign on behalf of the Cherokee Nation."

"They do not represent the Cherokee Nation." John argued. "I am the chief."

"They question your authority," Jackson leaned back in his chair, "you were appointed by Chief Pathkiller. You are being out-flanked by your own people." John shook his head.

"Can we Indians not live with the whites in peace? Surely that's what our constitution represents to defend rights of liberty and freedom."

"There are peaceful tribes. I believe the Cherokee are a noble tribe, but the Creek massacres have destroyed that peace. I will make you an offer of $200,000 dollars for two million acres of your lands."

John cleared his throat, trying hard to keep calm.

"The land is worth a lot more than this. There are also large deposits of gold. I cannot agree to this." John placed the 15000 signatures on the table.

"These are the over 15,000 signatures of ninety percent of the Cherokee people. How can Mr. Ridge be justified in his claim?"

President Jackson was not impressed, even by such a large number of signatures.

"We have passed the Indian Removal Act, that's all my government need!" John Ross was beginning to get angry and could not help raising his voice:

"But the treaty does not represent the Cherokee people! These are the signatures of the Cherokee Nation."

"My friend," said the President, "circumstances render it impossible that you can flourish in the midst of a civilized community. You have but one remedy within your reach, and that is to remove to the west. I made you an offer of $200,000, I suggest you take it."

"It is our land, it is not for sale, Mr. President!" John Ross was livid. 12.

John H. Eaton talked to John Ross, Sequoyah and John Wirt, outside his office.

"Mr. Ross, I regret to inform you that Mr. John Ridge is in Washington at this very moment talking to President Jackson about a treaty to hand over Cherokee lands. He has called his delegation the Ridge Party."

John Ross was utterly shocked.

"I cannot believe that he would betray us."

***

In May 1832 John Ridge and Elias Boudinot talked privately about the situation, with Supreme Court Justice John McClean.

"I am losing faith in John Ross." complained John Ridge. "If we are not careful we will have no lands east or west."

"Then take the reservation to the east," said McClean, "and appoint a delegate in Congress."

"That way we could vote John Ross out of power." said Ridge.

***

CHAPTER EIGHT

A receptionist handed a letter to John Ridge at his hotel. He opened it immediately and read:

"Request urgent meeting. John Ross."

So, John Ross and Sequoyah met with Elias Boudinot and John Ridge at the Capitol Hotel in Washington, and questioned their decision.

"Yes, it is true," said Ridge, "I and Elias had a meeting with the chief court justice John McClean, we agreed with him that we can no longer support your plan to save the Cherokee Nation."

"If we all do not stand together against Washington, they will destroy us." John Ross was dismayed.

"We have no rights," said Elias, "can you not see, Indian lands belong to the United States. The governor of Georgia is pressing for removal of all Indians. Some Indians may live in peace, but some of the tribes kill whites, there is fear among them."

"We can all live in peace, whatever the colour of their skin." John Ross was convinced. Elias shook his head:

"Washington does not see it that way, especially President Jackson. He wants to rid all eastern lands of this problem."

"Do we not have rights?" John raised his voice. "Have the Indians not lived here for thousands of years!"

"We belong to the United States now," Ridge seemed to claim defeat, "the final decision comes from Washington."

"There must be a compromise," John Ross insisted, "where Indians can live with whites." He could not understand why Ridge and Boudinot, being of Cherokee origin themselves, could want to betray their own people.

"We disagree," said Ridge, "we resign from this council, along with others that will come with us."

John Ross looked each of them in the eye, as if searching for some answer that way.

"Do you realise what this means," he said. "It is over a thousand miles to the

western states. Your plan means up-rooting women, children, old people, and forcing them to march across the American wilderness. It would be genocide; thousands will die of exposure and exhaustion!"

John Ridge and Elias Boudinot stood up and walked out silently. John Ross turned to Sequoyah:

"I want you to get signatures from every Cherokee. This list you will bring to Washington, it will be a petition to the president."

"It will take time." said Sequoyah.

"Make haste, Sequoyah," urged John. "It is the last hope for the Cherokee Nation." 13.

One month later, at John Ross's home in Georgia, Sequoyah brought a giant heavy leather-bound folder and placed it on John's desk. It was bound with leather string and 300 pages long. Sequoyah was very pleased with this.

"Here it is," he said, "15,423 signatures."

"That's ninety percent of the Cherokee Nation." John took this as great news.

He opened the folder and looked at the long line of names.

"It's like the first Cherokee census," he said, "it will be helpful, if we have to organise a move west."

***

John and Sequoyah made another long journey to Washington, to present the petition to President Jackson.

The President was writing at his desk when John Ross entered. He looked up and admitted:

"It's been a long time since we met."

"Mr. President," replied John, "thank you for seeing me."

"It's a very serious matter," said the President, "but we need to resolve it. I saw Mr. Ridge and Mr. Boudinot the other day. I can see that there is a split on policy in the Cherokee Nation. I have here a treaty, that they have agreed to sign on behalf of the Cherokee Nation."

"They do not represent the Cherokee Nation." John argued. "I am the chief."

"They question your authority," Jackson leaned back in his chair, "you were appointed by Chief Pathkiller. You are being out-flanked by your own people." John shook his head.

"Can we Indians not live with the whites in peace? Surely that's what our constitution represents to defend rights of liberty and freedom."

"There are peaceful tribes. I believe the Cherokee are a noble tribe, but the Creek massacres have destroyed that peace. I will make you an offer of $200,000 dollars for two million acres of your lands."

John cleared his throat, trying hard to keep calm.

"The land is worth a lot more than this. There are also large deposits of gold. I cannot agree to this." John placed the 15000 signatures on the table.

"These are the over 15,000 signatures of ninety percent of the Cherokee people. How can Mr. Ridge be justified in his claim?"

President Jackson was not impressed, even by such a large number of signatures.

"We have passed the Indian Removal Act, that's all my government need!" John Ross was beginning to get angry and could not help raising his voice:

"But the treaty does not represent the Cherokee people! These are the signatures of the Cherokee Nation."

"My friend," said the President, "circumstances render it impossible that you can flourish in the midst of a civilized community. You have but one remedy within your reach, and that is to remove to the west. I made you an offer of $200,000, I suggest you take it."

"It is our land, it is not for sale, Mr. President!" John Ross was livid. 14.

On December 29th, 1835 President Jackson and John Ridge had a discussion in the Oval Office of the White House.

"It is just another ploy to delay us." said Jackson.

"We must sign a treaty and force the Indian removal."

"I agree," said Ridge. "I have wasted enough time on this problem."

The Treaty of Encota was laid on the table. Jackson signed it along with other members of the Ridge party, John Ridge and Elias Boudinot.

Sequoyah rode up to the Capitol Hotel in Washington, where John Ross was staying, and hurried inside.

"Ridge and Boudinot have signed the Treaty of Encota." He told John Ross a little out of breath. John frowned:

"What treaty? The Cherokee Nation knows nothing about this."

"They call it Treaty of New Echota, giving up Cherokee lands for a few dollars!"

"At what price?" John was alarmed.

"At 10 cents an acre."

"It's about 10% of the actual value of the land!" John was furious. "This treaty has not been approved by the Cherokee council. $4.34 per acre, the going rate for land sold in the state of Georgia in 1835 was between $18.00 an acre and $25.00 an acre. This is criminal!" Sequoyah remained calm, at least on the outside.

"Ridge and Boudinot have signed their death warrant!"

***

CHAPTER NINE

When John Ross returned home to Georgia, he told his wife, Quatie.

"Today is the saddest day for the Cherokee Nation, for thousands of years we have lived in this land; now our own people have signed it away with one pen-stroke. A whole nation vanishes."

"What do we do now?" asked Quatie.

"We wait on Washington's next move!" said John.

Outside the Governors Building in Georgia, Andrew Lumkin stood in front of a packed audience, holding an auction hammer. Governor Toop looked on.

"Thank you, gentlemen," Lumkin began, "the lottery will commence. We are here today to sell off all Cherokee lands. This land lottery is a system of land re-distribution for Georgia's citizens. Under this system, qualifying citizens have registered for a chance to win lots of land that had formerly belonged to the Cherokee Indians and Creek Indians. Each lot marked on this map consists of frothy acres at a price of $40."

The auction went perfectly in the Governor's favour. In the Governors Building, Lumkin and Troop counted bundles of money.

"A very good day, Mr. Lumkin." said Troop with cheerful conceit. "This gold belt lots is very valuable, 85,000 people have competed for 18,309 land lots, and at least 133,000 people competed for 35,000 gold belt."

"Yes indeed," cheered Lumkin, "the profits will be high."

Two men arrived and Governor Troop greeted them. 15.

Another discussion took place in the Oval Office between President Jackson, Governor Troup and General Scott.

"We have to take action, Mr. President." started Governor Troup. "We have laid claim to Cherokee land. We have the Encota Agreement, but you need to give the order for the Indian Removal Act to be brought into force and make all this legal."

"Very well." The President nodded decisively. "We have waited two years to remove the Cherokee. The time for waiting is over."

Troop turned to General Scott:

"I want you to take one thousand soldiers and remove all Cherokee to the West to the territory of Oklahoma."

"I will carry out your orders, Mr. President." General Scott agreed. The President signed an order to activate the Indian Removal Act.

***

May 10, 1838 – at his headquarters in West Point, General Winfried Scott wrote a letter to John Ross:

"Dear Mr Ross, the President of the United States has sent me with a powerful army, to cause you, to obey the Treaty of New Echota, to join that part of your people who have already established in prosperity on the other side of the Mississippi. Every Cherokee man, woman and child in the state of Georgia, must be in motion to join their brethren in the far West. My friends!"

***

One thousand American soldiers ride on horseback across the countryside of Georgia. The carried the banner of the American flag. They were led by General Scott. The General told his army:

"This is no sudden determination on the part of the President, whom you and I must now obey. My troops already occupy many positions in the country that you are to abandon, and thousands and thousands are approaching from every quarter, to render resistance and escape alike hopeless. All those troops, regular and militia, are your friends. Receive them and confide in them as such. Obey them when they tell you that you can remain no longer in this country."

An Indian scout saw the army approaching. He jumped on his horse and galloped across the countryside towards John Ross's house. John came out on the porch with Quatie to meet him.

"What is it?" asked John.

"The America army are one their way," replied the scout, "about fifty miles east."

"Tell all the Indian chiefs to meet here tomorrow at noon." John instructed.

"Yes, Sir." The scout mounted his horse and galloped away. John Ross turned to his wife.

"The time has come, Quatie!"

***

On April 6, 1838, General Scott approached the Ross's house, followed by his army. John Ross and Quatie came out on the porch, along with their children. (In 1838 they would have been late teens, early 20's, not children) The General pulled in his horse. Without dismounting, he shouted:

"Mr. John Ross!"

"Yes," said John, "I am John Ross."

"I am here on President Jackson's orders." said Scott, remaining on his high horse. "I am here to enforce the treaty of Encota, signed by your people. I have one thousand soldiers with another six thousand ready in my barracks."

"I am the chosen Chief of the Cherokee Nation." John stood straight. "This treaty was never agreed by the Cherokee Nation council. I have fifteen thousand signatures that reject it."

"Let's be realistic, Mr. Ross," said Scott, arrogantly. "I have an army. We are here to do a job. I have my orders to clear these lands of all Cherokee Indians, in the next few weeks. I am not interested in political arguments, they are over. If you have been betrayed by your own people, then they can answer to you. You must leave your house immediately."

General Scott finally dismounted and pulled out a map. He unfolded it and showed it to John Ross.

"I want the Cherokee Nation immediately to be divided into three military districts. Within two weeks I want every Cherokee in North Georgia, Tennessee, Alabama to be captured. The Cherokee are to be rounded up."

John felt anger rise up, but his voice remained calm:

"Let me lead my own people!"

"What do you propose?" The General frowned.

"The Cherokee can be placed under my control. I will divide them into thirteen groups, led by their own men. I want no soldiers present. Let them leave peacefully."

"You have two weeks, Sir." Scott commanded without compassion. "If these lands are not clear of all Cherokee, any remaining Cherokee will be arrested and placed in stockades and I will get my men to escort them out of the territory and across the Mississippi."

***

The Baptist Church was packed, when John Ross addressed the congregation:

"My dear people, today, I met with General Scott. He has arrived with one thousand soldiers to force your removal. He has given me one month for all Cherokee lands to be cleared. You know that I have fought hard to prevent this, but some among us have signed the treaty of Encota and signed all these lands away. I have agreed with them that thirteen groups of people travel westward on four routes. I have come here today to tell you, to not resist these soldiers, your lives are in danger. Any Cherokee who remain on this land can be captured and imprisoned and possibly executed. I am looking for twelve men to volunteer to lead our people to Oklahoma. Pack whatever belongings you have, I will do my best to organise horses and wagons. The journey is over a thousand miles. Twelve men step forward Black, White and Indian." (black men were all slaves in 1838)

Elijah Hicks, Hair Conrad, Daniel Colton, Rev. Jesse Bushyhead, Rev. S. Foreman, Choowalooka, Moses Daniel, James Brown, Rev. Butrick, George Hicks, John Drew, Richard Taylor and Peter Hilderbrand all stood up and came forward.

"The white men among you are not obliged to join us on this difficult journey. You are white, you are safe in these lands now."

"No," Richard Taylor shook his head. "I cannot abandon you and your people. There are fifteen thousand among you. You will need all the help you can get. The Lord is on our side."

John Ross looked around the crowded congregation, packed with Cherokee and many white people. Daniel Colton stepped forward:

"I will lead also."

"Count me in." said Sequoyah.

"I will gladly be one of you." Moses Daniel volunteered.

"You will need a priest," said the Rev. Butrick, "count me in, too."

"It will be a long and difficult journey." John Ross continued. "But if you want to live you must leave this land. If you do not, you will be rounded up or possibly shot. The journey is over one thousand miles through difficult territory, mountains, rivers and swamps. But we have no option but to travel, women and children will stay in the wagons. The men will walk or travel on horseback. It is a very emotional moment. The choir sing Amazing Grace." 17.

At night in the church twelve men gathered around, including John Ross, Elijah Hicks, Hair Conrad, Daniel Colton, Rev. Jesse Bushyhead, Rev. S. Foreman, Choowalooka, Moses Daniel, James Brown, George Hicks, John Drew, Richard Taylor, Peter Hilderbrand. They all looked at a large map.

"There is the land route and the water route," John Ross began, "down the Tennessee River by flatboat, then south on the Mississippi to the Arkansas River. It's about one thousand miles. Then follow this river to Fort Smith, on the border between Arkansas and Indian Territory. From here you can head northwest to the area reserved for the Cherokee in Oklahoma. The land Route begins at Rattlesnake Springs and heads northwest to the vicinity of Nashville, Tennessee, then to Hopkinsville, Kentucky. From here crossing the Ohio river just northwest of the Tennessee river. From here the Cherokee move southwest, crossing the Mississippi near Cape Girardeau. From here the route heads south-southwest across the Ozark plateau to the Oklahoma Territory."

***

CHAPTER ELEVEN

The following day, they assembled. Elijah Hicks, Hair Conrad, Daniel Colton, Rev. Jesse Bushyhead, Rev. S. Foreman, Choowalooka, Moses Daniel, James Brown, George Hicks, John Drew, Richard Taylor, Peter Hilderbrand. The thirteen men rode out along with John Ross. John and Quatie along with Sequoyah rode across the countryside at speed to a group of tepees and huts. Indians packed wagons and horses.

Campfires were built at night for the group to eat and rest, as well as to gather more people to follow. Sequoyah stayed with John and Quatie.

"We are running out of time." he said.

"Scott gave me four weeks," John told them.

"We have few wagons and horses." said Sequoyah. "Many will have to walk."

"There are not enough of horses and wagons." Moses Daniel confirmed. "There is no way that we can meet this deadline of the white chief. Many refuse to go, especially the old women and children."

John Ross sighed.

"Tell the people we have to go. It is too dangerous to stay. They will kill us."

"It's over one thousand miles," said Quatie. "There is little water."

"We can maybe walk fifty miles a day." said John.

"The old and the sick cannot walk that far." Quatie reminded him.

"Forty days at fifty miles a day."

"We have no chance if the winter comes," Quatie continued, "many will die." 18.

Elias Boudinot was busy supervising the removal of printing presses and books from the Cherokee Phoenix office. John Ross entered the building without knocking.

"We need to talk." he demanded.

Boudinot sat down at his desk, surrounded by packed cases and lit a cigar.

"You're travelling west?" asked John.

"Yes, I am following the terms of the Encota Treaty." Boudinot casually puffed his cigar, as if it was no big matter.

"Write to Washington and revoke the treaty!" John urged him. "People are going to die, Elias, because of your treaty. It's not the will of the Cherokee people. Only 500 signed, I have 15,000 signatures."

"I am a realist John; the white man does not want us here. You know that I have tried to civilize the Cherokee. I have built churches and schools and adopted white man's ways. We do not belong here anymore. I have signed my death warrant, but I believe it is for the good of the Cherokee."

"I was offered two hundred thousand dollars," John was determined to convince him. "You sold Cherokee lands for nothing."

"It's the best deal I could do." said Elias.

"The best deal for millions of acres." John Ross raised his voice. "Where is our new deeds for lands in Oklahoma, where is the money?"

Elias took out a large scroll and opened it, spreading it out on the desk, so they both could see it clearly.

"This is the new land in Oklahoma." he explained. "The money will be sent to us when we arrive." John Ross could not believe what he just heard. Was this man really so naive, as to trust the governors promise of money and land?

"What guarantee have we?" John argued. "The American government have broken all their treaties with the Indians."

***

John had no intention of giving up. He returned to the Baptist Church and spoke to the Rev. Butrick and Sequoyah.

"I want you, Sequoyah, to draw up a list of all people who will travel to Oklahoma. I want every name of every woman, child and man. I don't want to lose track of anyone on this treacherous journey."

"This is going to be a difficult task." said Sequoyah. "I will use the signatures of the Cherokee; we have already taken."

"Ok, I will get some men to help you. I want you to draw up a list for each of the twelve men, from your records. They will go first. I and my group will wait until the end. Until I know that all the Cherokee have safely left." Sequoyah met John Ross outside his house.

"Have you found the boat builders?" he asked.

"Yes," John told him. "Tokpa and his African slaves are carpenters. They want to come with us and live as free men in the West. But we have little money. So, they offer to work for free. How much money have we left?"

"Five hundred and sixty dollars." said Sequoyah. "The money never arrived from the government." A dark shadow cast over John's face. He knew all along the government was going to let them down.

"Let me worry about the money." he said. "Get all the carpenters together by the boat house on the river."

***

Topka and his carpenters assembled in the boathouse. Tokpa was a broad strong African man with big strong hands. Sequoyah introduced him and the carpenters to John Ross. Tokpa's daughter Campu was also with them. John laid plans of boats on a large makeshift wooden table.

"Mr. Ross," said Tokpa. "We are at your service."

"We need boats," John instructed, "at least twelve and we need them in one month."

"We can build really fast, boss." Tokpa was enthusiastic. "We will build the best boats."

"Where did you learn to build?" John was curious.

"In Africa on the Ivory Coast. We were taken from there and put in chains." Tokpa held up his arms and John noticed a brand on his wrists.

"What is it?"

"My boss he branded me. We escaped from Alabama. We cannot go back, we come with you and we help re build the Cherokee nation."

"How many are you?"

"Twenty-five."

"Ok you can come." John agreed. "The new Cherokee nation will be free to all men."

"My people will be grateful to you." Tokpa smiled broadly. "We will build the best boats for you." John leaned over the table and the slaves gathered round to listen as he described the work ahead.

"I want these flatboats fifty-five feet long by sixteen broads. Rectangular in shape and flat-bottomed, they will be constructed of green oak plank, with no nails or iron. The heavy oak planks will be fastened by wooden pins to still heavier frames of timber. The seams are originally caulked with pitch or tar. They will have boarded sides three feet high. Even fully loaded, they drew only about three feet of water. For navigation, we will have rigged with sweeps on the sides, a rudder or steering-oar, and a short front sweep. We will have a shelter with a cooking area. They will be covered in canvas."

"We will do our best, sir." said Campu. "We will work day and night. So long as we have the wood, we will be no delays."

"We are cutting down trees and will deliver in two days."

The following day many slaves were hard at work in the forest, with giant axes. Eventually they hauled logs along the road, pulled by horses to the boathouse. Here they began to work tirelessly, building the giant flatboats.

John and Sequoyah inspected one of the nearly finished products.

"It looks like Noah's Ark." said John. Sequoyah smiled: The fourteen boats were launched on the Tennessee river.

At night in the Baptist Church, John Ross was looking at a giant map of the Mississippi. Sequoyah arrived with Jesse Bushyhead and Doctor Nielsen. He was a polite young man with fair hair, fair complexion and round spectacles.

"I have found a doctor!" said Sequoyah.

"Pleased to meet you." Dr. Nielsen introduced himself.

"Please sit down." said John. "Thank you for volunteering."

"Rev. Butrick sent a message," the Doctor told them. "I am based in Chatoonoga. You will need my help, there is smallpox and cholera, it has killed many Indians already." John felt a little downcast:

"I think the cold may kill us first."

Doctor Nielsen continued with grave news:

"I received a report this morning, that over six hundred and forty-three Indians have been killed by American soldiers. How many days have we left?"

"Three days," confirmed John. "We have run out of time. The Indians are sleeping in the church. Five hundred and fifty-three, the last of the Cherokee Nation in the East."

The sun rose and daylight began to filter through the church windows. Dr. Nielsen, Sequoyah and John Ross walked among the sleeping Indians lying on the church floor. Quatie said some prayers at the altar, which was covered in candles.

"This is Doctor Nielsen." John introduced them. "This is my wife, Quatie."

"Pleased to meet you." said the Doctor. Quatie looked up at him, with hope in her eyes.

"It's good you came; I have many sick people here. They have a long journey ahead. Some are not able to travel."

"I totally disapprove of the government action." said Doctor Nielsen. "It's barbaric!"

"We must look to the future." said John.

"We Indians own this land," said Quatie, "we are being forced out of here. These people do not deserve this."

"Have faith, Quatie." John tried to comfort his wife. "We will re-build a new Cherokee nation in the West. The medicine men have prophesied that seven generations from now the Cherokee will rise again."

***

CHAPTER TWELVE

Sequoyah was riding across the Tennessee countryside, when he saw American soldiers rounding up Indians. He galloped towards them.

"What are you doing?" he called over to them.

"We have orders from General Scott to put these Indians in stockades and then escort them to the border!" replied one of the soldiers.

"We had an agreement." Sequoyah reminded him. The soldier was determined to carry out the General's orders.

"Your time is up!" he said rudely. "Tell Mr. Ross that any Indians in these lands from 12 o'clock tomorrow will be arrested."

***

Over 400 Cherokee men, women, and children were held in confinement before beginning the trip west. Sequoyah returned to Rossville to meet with John Ross.

"General Scott and his men have begun the clearance," Sequoyah reported, "and are rounding up our people and putting them in stockades."

"But what about our agreement?" John was furious at the government having broken its promise yet again.

"The solider says our time is up." said Sequoyah. "We are three days from the border, we should have left by now."

"What about the twelve leaders?"

"They are ready to go." confirmed Sequoyah. John Ross was determined to negotiate:

"Ok, let me talk to General Scott."

Sequoyah knew where to find General Scott. So, he and John rode out to the water creek to his camp.

"What can I do for you?" asked the General, already knowing the answer.

"You are rounding up my people." John complained. General Scott shrugged:

"The month is up, the land is not cleared, it's at least three days travel to the border."

"You cannot put people in stockades," John tried to reason with the General. "What about food and water? This will destroy them! You should release them and wait until this hot sun cools down. There is no water, the people will die, the wells have dried up."

General Scott showed no mercy or compassion.

"Any Indians already in stockades will remain under arrest. Do you understand?"

"But these women and children will die in this summer heat, without water or food." John was in despair.

"Then tell your leaders to get organized." The General commanded. "I have seen no real proof of the removal. Good day, sir."

"This is not civilized!" John raised his voice, infuriated by the General's inhumanity.

Captain Hyde and Captain Brown stand before Governor Troup in his office. The Governor began to speak quietly, his voice getting louder as he continued:

"I have heard from General Scott. The Indians have been rounded up and put in stockades, but some ain't moving. I want you to get your men and ride out there. Use any means possible to make sure they are out of Georgian territory."

***

In the wooded hills near a small Indian village church Georgian gunman led by Captain Hyde prepared in hiding to attack. They lined up on horseback. At Captain Hyde's order they galloped towards the trading post.

The Captain was ready for some challenges when carrying out the Governor's orders, but he and his gunmen had not expected to be up against Cherokee warriors in war paint, some with guns and some with bows and arrows, all ready to defend themselves and their land.

Captain Hyde killed a Cherokee trying to shut the gates. Warriors passed through. Indians fought in a pitched bloody battle killing and injuring many soldiers. But the soldiers outnumbered them and eventually overran them.

Sequoyah rode up to John Ross's house and reported:

"Hired gunmen are attacking Indian villages!"

John Ross urgently mounted his horse:

"Let's ride out there."

John and Sequoyah arrived at the scene on horseback. They saw Indian men picking up wounded comrades and retreating for cover under a hail of gunfire and arrows. The killing fields began to clear. Through the haze, John saw men lying dead.

A mass grave was dug outside the stockade. Rev. Butrick said some prayers by the graves of one hundred Indians.

***

In Rossville, Sequoyah sat at a desk, along with five other Indian clerks. Indians moved in line, passing them, giving them their name. An Indian named Tsali came to the top of the queue.   With him was his ten-year-old daughter Talita.

"I want to speak to chief John Ross." said Tsali.

"Brother, why?" asked Sequoyah.

"I refuse to leave the land of my fathers."

"How many are you?"

"Over one thousand." said Tsali. Sequoyah got up.

"Come with me."

Tsali and Talita followed Sequoyah to John Ross's office. John looked up from his desk, tired and worn.

"Please sit down."

They sat.

"What is your name?" asked John.

"I am Tsali," replied the man, "and this is my daughter, Talita."

"How can I help you?"

"I refuse to leave," Tsali told him with determination in his voice. "The Cherokee people have lived in these lands for thousands of years."

"If you do not leave you will be arrested." said John. "Where are you from?"

"Quallatown, Carolina. I will take my people to the mountains; we will hide in the forests. This is our land."

"Yes, it is," John agreed, "but some of our own Cherokee have betrayed us and signed a treaty with the whites. I must warn you that if you do not go, you will have little protection from the whites."

"I come to ask you to speak to the white chiefs." Tsali implored. John sighed:

"I have had many meetings with the white chiefs, but they will not listen to us."

"Then I will go to the mountains." Tsali decided. John got up from his seat as Tsali rose.

"Tsali, my friend," he said gravely, "your family is in great danger."

"If we leave this land," Tsali insisted, "you betray the memory of the great Cherokee leaders and warriors that lived here for thousands of years. The people think only of the love we have for our land. We will never let go; it will be like leaving our mother that gave us birth." Tsali turned and left with his daughter. 22.

General Scott paced up and down the room in his headquarters. General Foster brought the news that: (Can't find anything on General Foster. There are several on Google, but all at a later period. A first name would help to find this one).

"Tsali, the Indian chief has escaped into the forest in North Georgia with one thousand of his tribe. He refuses to leave Georgia."

"I want this Cherokee Indian arrested!" said Scott.

"I will organise the seventh Calvary and the help of Indians scouts, to find him." said General Foster.

Meanwhile, Tsali and his family were traveling through the beautiful forest towards a cave. The light streamed through the trees. General Foster and his men galloped across the Carolina countryside.

Tsali and his extended family had found shelter in a large cave and gathered around a fire. They heard horses outside. They began to fire at the soldiers from their hideout and killed some of them.

***

CHAPTER THIRTEEN

In his office, John Ross talked to an Indian named Yonahuska.

"Tsali has killed many soldiers." Yonahuska told him.

"We cannot have Indians killing soldiers." said John. "The army could adopt a shoot to kill policy and put more lives in danger."

"I will track him down." suggested Yonahuska.

***

In the forest Tsali found himself surrounded by Yonahuska and his Cherokee braves. He tried to escape. He was shot and fell bleeding to the ground. Yonahuska knelt down beside him. Tsali spoke his last words:

"We are the 'Warriors of the Rainbow', spread the message. Teach them how to live the 'Way of the Great Spirit'. The world today has turned away from the Great Spirit and that is why our Earth is 'Sick'. The 'Warriors of the Rainbow' would show the peoples that the Great Spirit is full of love and understanding, and will teach them how to make the Earth beautiful again. The Warriors of the Rainbow will teach the people of the ancient practices of Unity, Love and Understanding. They will teach of Harmony among people in all four corners of the Earth. Never to destroy for the furtherance of greed, the white man has taken our lands and have abused their power. The Great Spirit will help us to find the way ....." With those wise words Tsali died in Yonahuska's arms.

***

By April, 5, 1838, John Ross and his family were now living in a tent. Moses Daniel met up with John and Sequoyah to discuss the next steps. He reported:

"General Scott and his army have forced some of the Indians to leave. I have a telegram." He handed the telegram to John, who read it:

"Captain Deas, U. S. Army is heading for the border with 1250 Cherokee. Lt. Whitley, U. S. Army, 800 Cherokee - Capt. Drane, 1070 Cherokee. John Ridge, 650 Cherokee. Leader - John Benge, 1,1003. So, it looks like John Ridge is part of this forced removal."

"There was shortage of drinking water." said Sequoyah. "In addition, the season of fever had set in. The three detachments that left under army control, all left from Ross Landing, the first on June 6, the second on June 15, and the third on June 17. The first two detachments went by water, but the water level had fallen so low that the third group went by wagons to Waterloo, Alabama. The Cherokee were forcibly placed on a steamboat, guarded by twenty-three guards, in order to prevent escape." John shook his head in disgust, then ordered:

"Get the twelve leaders together, we must move fast!"

***

In June 1838 the Cherokee Indian Council gathered in the Baptist Church. Elijah Hicks, Hair Conrad, Daniel Cooper, Rev. Jesse Bushyhead, Rev. S. Foreman, Choowalooka, Moses Daniel, James Brown, George Hicks, John Drew, Richard Taylor amd Peter Hilderbrand all looked at a giant map spread out on the table. John Ross started the conversation:

"Sequoyah brought me news this morning that there was a forced removal by General Scott and John Ridge. At least four thousand are being marched west. General Scott captured Alabama and Georgian Cherokees. How is your preparation, have you put together your lists with Sequoyah?" The men placed their list in bundles on the table. John began to do some maths.

"That's 11,031 Cherokee. How many horses and wagons do we have?"

"Five thousand horses," Sequoyah confirmed. "And 654 wagons, each drawn by six horses."

"That's not enough!" said John.

"That is all we have!"

"My people," continued John, "504 in total, will travel by boat."

"Boats," said Sequoyah, "but we have no boats."

"Then we will build them," John decided. "There are many carpenters among the Cherokee and slaves." (The slaves already built and launched boats in a previous chapter!)

"It is hundreds of miles down the river." Sequoyah reminded. "It is very dangerous."

"I have no choice," said John ruefully, "there are no horses, my friend. I will go last. I want all of the Cherokee except my people to go first. I want you all to be ready to go by November 4th. (check all those dates – very confusing). It is not the best time, as the winter is upon us but we have no choice. I will go by the river route and then by land. We cannot force women and children to walk one thousand miles with no wagons. I have made arrangements for food and other necessities."

"I have found volunteers among them." said Sequoyah.

"The invasion of the whites has caused panic among the Indians."

***

On the 4th of November 1838 thousands of Indians and hundreds of wagons gathered at Chattonooga. John Ross stood before a small church on high steps. Quatie and the Rev. Butrick stood by his side. John announced:

"My dear people, the day has come for us to leave our homeland. A homeland that has belonged to the Cherokee Indians for thousands of years. I know that you all leave with heavy hearts. The journey will not be an easy one, especially for the women and children and the older among you. I want you to know that I have done all I possibly can to save this great nation and the lands of the Cherokee. We have been promised 50,000 acres of land in the West, by the government in Oklahoma that will become your new homeland. I will stay here until I know that all Cherokee have been able to leave and are safe. Let us now say a prayer for Tsali and his family who died some weeks ago. Tsali believed in the homeland, but he fought the whites. He will be always remembered by the Cherokee as a martyr and the one who made the ultimate sacrifice. I ask you to follow the path of peace in your new lives. As you cross America do not provoke the

whites, do not take up arms and always follow the peaceful way. God bless you all. Let us now pray to God for his deliverance."

***

John and Quatie watched a large caravan of wagons and Cherokee on horseback, slowly moving through the Chattonooga countryside. Some were walking, others carried children in their arms. John's eyes filled with tears. At night, back in his tent, John wrote in his diary.

''The newly built boats were launched on the Tennessee River. Hundreds of Cherokee boarded the boats. The slaves were organised by Tokpa. Food was carried on board in boxes of all sizes, bound to the deck by ropes''.

Doctor Nielsen and Quatie boarded the flatboats. Sequoyah checked the list counting the Indians and the slaves.

"We are ready, sir."

John walked over to the church door. His parents, Daniel and Molly Ross arrived.

"We are ready to go with you." said Daniel. John turned towards the boats and lifted his arm.

"Cast off!" called Sequoyah. The slaves cast off the ropes of each boat. John and Quatie ran up the last gangplank with tears in their eyes. Within minutes the strong current carried all the twelve boats downstream. Tokpa steered the flatboat at the rear.

"I hope this boat is strong enough." said John.

"Dont worry, boss," Tokpa assured him. "I have built this boat like a piece of steel."

"How far can we travel in one day?" asked John.

"Maybe thirty miles," said Tokpa, "depending on the current." Quatie hurried.

"We have a sick girl on board." she said. Doctor Nielsen examined the girl, who was breathing heavily.

"She has pneumonia." The Doctor diagnosed. (How old is the girl? Toddler? Teenager?)

"Very little we can do," said Quatie sadly. "Keep her warm and hope the fever dies down."

At night John Ross was at the stern with Tokpa, looking across to the shoreline where lights flickered. John was concerned.

"We must be careful not to hit any sandbanks or rocks."

"Don't worry boss. I have been down this river man times."

"It's a long way to Oklahoma." John lifted his lamp and opened up a map of the river route.

"We are heading north about five hundred miles. We will pass Gunters Landing, Fort Payne, Tuscumbia, Waterloo, Florence and Green Ferry. Then we turn south on the Mississsppi River another five hundred miles. It's one thousand miles to Little Rock."

Tokpa was always positive:

"We will get there."

"It's the winter that worries me," John was being realistic. "Very soon the snow and ice will come. The rivers can get frozen over." Tokpa sounded his big brass bell. One by one all the boats replied. It was a very errie sound crossing the river. Nielsen, the doctor hurried up.

"Come inside." John followed him into the boat. By the lamp they could see the face of a young Cheroke girl, struggling to breathe.

"She is still very sick." the doctor confirmed. Quatie called them. They looked over to the other side of the cabin. Quatie leaned over an old Cherokee man. Doctor Nielsen examined him.

"He's dead." he concluded and closed the old man's eyes.

In the morning, the old Cherokee was wrapped in canvas and tied with rope. Rev. Butrick said the final prayers:

"God have mercy, and we now commit his body to the waters. Grant him eternal rest, O Lord. And let perpetual light shine upon him and into the halls of the heavenly banquet. Lord, in your mercy ..."

Quatie put her arm around the Cherokee's wife to comfort her, as they watched the body being slid into the waters of the river.

***

CHAPTER FOURTEEN

In the cabin John, Quatie and the Rev. Butrick warmed themselves with some soup and bread. John was tired.

"How many more will die?" He muttered.

"Remember are words of St. Mathew." said the Rev. Butrick. "Those who endure to the end will be saved."

"How much endurance do we Cherokee need?" John replied. "Have we not suffered enough?"

"In these dark hours we need to have faith," the Minister continued. "Faith will carry us through. We must have faith. We must look deep inside our hearts and souls and find the strength to go on."

John had his doubts that faith was enough, when God did not seem to listen to their prayers.

"I have fought long and hard for these people. But their struggle is of biblical proportions. Is there any justice in the world? Do the Christian whites believe in justice? Have they lost their God and greed has become their only value they pursue?"

"They will pay for their greed." The Rev. Butrick was convinced.

"We will build a new nation with values of honest trust respect." said John. "The Cherokee Nation will become an example to all."

The Tennessee River was difficult to navigate, owing to the drought, drying up wells and springs. River travel was arduous, if not impossible because of low river levels due to the drought.

"I never heard of Gunter's Landing," said Sequoyah. John explained: 25.

On December 6th, 1838 the boats arrived at Gunther's Landing. The flat boats dropped anchor, by the timber jetty. John Gunther (describe) and his Cherokee wife Ghigoneli greeted and welcomed them.

"We heard you were coming." said Gunther.

"Can we can come ashore?" John Ross asked, carefully.

"This is Alabama, not Georgia." said Gunther. "You are all welcome. This is my Cherokee wife, Ghigonelli."

"My people need water badly." said John.

Tokpa ordered his slaves to help the Cherokee off the boats.

"You carry slaves, too?" Gunther frowned.

"They are not slaves now," John explained. "They are free men and are under my protection."

"They will come to no harm." Gunther assured him.

***

In John Gunther's house a buffet was laid on a large table with enough food for everyone to eat.

"A party of Cherokee passed this way a few weeks back." John Gunther told John Ross.

"Who were they?" John Ross wanted to know.

"A party of 466 Cherokees," said Gunther. "Elias Boudinot and Major Ridge and his wife and was under the charge of Dr. John S. Young, and the physician Dr. C. Lillybridge, plus three assistants and three interpreters, one of whom was Elijah Hicks."

"These men destroyed the Cherokee Nation." John scowled. "How many were there?"

"They travelled by steamboat to Knoxville." Gunther carried on. "I do not agree with Indian removal. You have a long journey ahead. That river goes on forever."

"Jackson destroyed the Cherokees." John raised his voice. Gunther was angry with the President, too.

"I have met the man I agree. I will stay here to protect the Indians. Your people will be safe in the barn tonight."

Quatie spoke to Gunther's wife:

"You must come and visit in Oklahoma when we get settled."

"We would be happy to see you." Ghigoneli agreed. Just then Doctor Nielsen arrived and John enquired how everyone was keeping.

"The children have measles," the Doctor reported with some alarm, "pains in the abdomen, high fever, influenza, headache, a number of children complaining of common colds." Sequoyah and Tokpa joined them.

"I advise you to go to Tscumbia and try and get a steamer." Gunther suggested. "I'ts a journey of eight hundred miles by river to Little Rock. Your little boats will not survive such a journey. Very soon the river will be covered in ice."

"We have little money to pay for such a trip." said John. Gunther got up and went outside. In a few minutes he returned with a steel box. Without speaking, he lifted the lid, took two thousand dollars out of the box and handed the money to John Ross. John looked at the money in disbelief.

"John Ridge gave it to me for supplies and horses." Gunther explained. "It is blood money as far as I am concerned. Take it, I don't want money that Ridge and his people obtained by dishonest means."

The following morning John Ross and his group prepared to leave, thanking John Gunther for his generosity.

"Good bye, my friend." said John.

"Goodbye, my friend." returned Gunther. Quatie and Ghigoneli also said good bye. 26.

Out of the mist appeared Tscumbia one early morning. The last outpost on the Tennessee river for five (5 what?) Small boats were moored on the riverbank. Alongside a small steam ship with one funnel. John Ross went on shore followed by Tokpa. A boatman greeted John:

"Where have you come from?"

"Ross's Point," replied John. "Is the captain on board?"

"Yes," acknowledged the boatman. They followed him up the gangplank. Suddenly a large grey-bearded man stood before them.

"My name is John Ross Chief of the Cherokee Nation." John introduced himself.

"Come beneath deck." said the Captain. John did as he asked.

"What can I do for you?" the Captain enquired.

"I have three hundred Indians with me." said John. "We need passage down the Tennessee river and then the Mississippi."

"That's a journey of one thousand miles." The Captain was astonished.

"My boats will not cover that distance and many of my people are sick."

"How sick are they?" The Captain frowned.

"Measles, Pneumonia," Dr. Nielsen started. The Captain was concerned:

"That is a risk to my crew. It's going to cost. I can only offer you the hold. No Indians or slaves on deck. I don't want no trouble with white passengers, fifty dollars a person."

"That's 2000 dollars." said Dr. Nielsen.

"Yes," confirmed the Captain, "this steamship ain't cheap and in cash, gentlemen." John took a bundle of notes from his bag and counted the money out.

***

CHAPTER FIFTEEN

The Cherokee struggled on board, to the ship's hold. The giant funnel belched smoke and a large fog horn was sounded. The ship sailed slowly down the Tennessee River. One thousand miles of water lay ahead, with very few places to stop; Memphis and Little Rock. The water and the food were rationed. But as the days went on, more and more Indians started to become ill with fever and measles. The cramped conditions of the hold were really too much to bear. The days and nights got colder. Then one day, John noticed that Quatie lay motionless and her eyes vacant. He was concerned for his wife's health.

"Quatie, are you ok?"

"I don't feel too good." she replied.

"Where is your shawl?"

"I gave it to one of the children." said Quatie.

"You will freeze to death."

"What about the children?"

John took off his coat and placed it over Quatie.

"I will get Doctor Nielsen." he said. He got up and returned within a few minutes with the Doctor.

Doctor Nielsen examined Quatie. Her laboured breathing gave him concern, and John was getting worried.

"What is it, doc?"

"It's pneumonia."

"What can we do?"

"Not a lot," the Doctor said gravely. "Keep her warm and give her hot soup."

From that day forward Quatie never recovered. From day to day John could

see her become weaker and weaker. The ship passed Memphis. After that, all was endless waters stretching on and on into the distance. John worried about the other Cherokee, where were they? They had no word. They experienced the coldest weather they had ever known anywhere. The streams were all frozen ice. On the Mississippi river numerous quantities of ice came floating down the river every day. Quatie's health contuined to decline.

***

On a cold dark night, John, Sequoyah, Doctor Nielsen and Tokpa gathered around Quatie, and their children Jane, James and Allen. Quatie coughed and breathed heavily. She looked up at her husband with watery eyes.

"John, I don't think I can go on."

"Darling Quatie, you can." John tried to convince her.

"No, John, I feel the great spirit wants to take me. You're a good man, John, our people need you. I just don't have the strength to go on. The price of our freedom has been very high. Children, you must be strong and take care of your father."

The fog horn blasted across the waters, as the ship reached Little Rock, Arkansas. John Ross leaned over the rails. Quatie's body was carried on shore. The Captain called to speak to John:

"I cannot take you any further. The river is frozen along its banks."

"Thank you for taking us this far." said John humbly.

"I am sorry for your loss." said the Captain and meant it.

"Thank you."

A shallow grave was dug in the frozen ground by Little Rock. Quatie was laid into the earth in the clothes she had passed away in. John and his family and many Indians gathered around the grave. John was deeply distressed by his wife's death. (What happened to the other people who died on board the ship?)

***

Supplies were needed urgently. John Ross talked with a store agent. He was with Rev. Butrick and Doctor Nielsen.

"I need horses and wagons."

"That's going to cost." said the agent. "How many?"

"Thirty wagons and two hundred horses."

The agent did some calculations and came up with a sum of $2,000 dollars.

"I don't have that kind of money." said John desperately. The agent was abrupt and without compassion:

"Sorry, I cannot help you."

As they walked down the street Rev. Butrick discovered a Baptist church across the road.

"I have an idea." He called out. The others followed him across the road. They entered the church and watched a black Baptist minister praying at the altar. The Rev. Butrick walked up to the minister, who introduced himself as the Rev. James.

"Can we talk?" asked Butrick.

"Yes," he replied, "just praying to the lord."

"I am a Baptist minister from Tennessee. This is John Ross chosen chief of the Cherokee." John Ross continued:

"We have travelled one thousand miles down the Tennessee and Mississippi, but the river is now frozen ahead. We have 500 Indians!"

"Where are you heading for?"

"Oklahoma!"

"Yes," the Rev. James looked very serious. "We have heard that you were coming this way. Many folks thought you had drowned or the flat boats had sunk."

"Have you heard news of the Cherokee?" The black minister remembered hearing something:

"There was news that there were Cherokee in their thousands, passing north of here. Where are your people?"

"Camped by the river," John told him, "but they will die in the cold if we do not get them inside soon."

The Rev. James nodded:

"This is the house of God, bring them here. They can stay in this church."

"I will bring them." said Sequoyah and left the church.

"Come back to my rooms and have some food." suggested the Rev. James.

***

There was a large dark wooden desk in the Rev. James's room, which was covered with bibles and candles.

"So how you plan on getting on?" asked James. John Ross took a deep breath and replied honestly:

"We have no wagons; we have run out of money. The money promised from the government did not arrive."

"Well, my church can lend you the money." The Rev. James did not see this as a problem. After all it was what the church was for. Christians were meant to help their fellow men in need. "How much do you need?"

"Two thousand dollars." said John. The Rev. James nodded and went over to a small safe behind the desk and opened it. He took out out five thousand dollars, and handed the money to John.

"The church does not charge interest."

***

At night Indians were lying on the church floor. John Ross, Sequoyah, Doctor Nielsen and the Rev. Butrick poured over a map.

"We have another five hundred miles to Oklahoma." said John. "We follow the riverbank to Spinona Bluff to Fort Smith, then on to Tallulah, Oklahoma."

The Cherokee and slaves sat up, looking towards the altar where Rev. James, Rev. Butrick, Doctor Nielsen, Tokpa, Sequoyah and John and his three adult children stood before them. John addressed the large group.

"I would like to thank the Rev. James for allowing us refuge in his church. I am sure more would have died in this bitter cold if we had not received his kind help. We have five hundred miles to go. Rev James and his church has provided the money for wagons and horses and food supplies. I know that you all have been through a lot of pain and suffering. But I ask you to have faith, that God's grace is with you all. We must not lose hope or lose spirit. Whatever the trials and tribulations, like Moses had when he left Egypt for the promised land. That promised land is there waiting for you. There has been some news that some of the Cherokee have passed north of here some weeks back, so you will be with them all soon. I ask you now to pray for the dead who have died on this journey and also for my wife Quatie." They all bowed their head.

***

CHAPTER SIXTEEN

At the edge of Little Rock Town, the Rev. James said goodbye to John Ross. The horses moved forward. John was thinking sadly.

"My children were deeply saddened by the death of their mother. A black slave named Bessie began a new job of their surrogate mother. The little one Jane did not speak for weeks with shock. It was pitiful to behold the women & children who suffered exceedingly as they were all obliged to walk. We have thunder showers sometimes two or three every day. In rare cases, the rain did come, sometimes violently. The thunder showers were unusually violent, one of its bolts struck very near. On the summits of the mountains red patches are frequently seen in the woods where the lightnings strike. We arrived at Lewisburg on the sixth day."

***

The wagons had nearly reached Lewisburg, Arkansas, when they all came to a halt. In front of them were ten men, all holding shot guns pointing them. John on his horse slowly moved forward.

"We come in peace," he said. "We are travelling to Oklahoma."

One of the gunmen, probably the gang leader, pointed his shotgun directly at John. He was rough and unkempt and his voice was coarse.

"We want no Indians or Negroes around here."

"We only want to stop for some water." said John. The gunman had no mercy:

"You cannot enter our town, travel on the north road."

"We have travelled hundreds of miles..." The gunman shot at the horse's feet, and threatened:

"You heard me!"

John beckoned Sequoyah to guide the wagons north.

***

In general, the white settlers who witnessed the Cherokee moving west were indifferent to their plight. While some did offer assistance, most did not. In a number of cases the settlers did not want the Cherokee in their towns, so the groups were forced to change their route. City fathers, who were unhappy with the long lines of Indians passing through town asked that they cross two miles north.

Eventually they arrived at the town of Spinona Bluff. The sun was clouded, no rain fell, the thunder rolled away and seemed hushed in the distance. It was hot in the beginning and they drank water from the streams when they came upon them. Many people slept on the ground, and they gathered wood to build campfires for cooking meals and to keep warm.

When it began to rain the roads were very muddy. Wagons got stuck and some people threw away their belongings to make the load lighter for the horses and oxen. Many people became ill and died. An account of one traveller who passed several Cherokee groups on his way west, testified to the severity of the rain and cold.

They camped in the forest for the night by the roadside under a severe fall of rain accompanied by heavy wind. Many of the old Indians were suffering extremely from the fatigue of the journey, and the ill health consequent upon it. Several then were quite ill, and an aged man was then in the last struggles of death.

***

After many weeks they arrived at Fort Smith. The sick and feeble were carried in wagons. Some travelled, with heavy burdens, with no shoes for the feet, except what nature had given them. Not only was the autumn wet, it was also unusually cold. The weather also became very cold, and wagons were covered with snow in the morning.

After another long and arduous journey, the depleted group reached Fort Gibson. They had now been on the road from Arkansas seventy-five days and had travelled five hundred and twenty-nine miles. Although many had not survived, John Ross had kept his faith. He believed they had been 'greatly favoured by the kind hand of providence of our heavenly father.' They had met with no serious accident and had been detained only two days by bad weather. It had, however, been exceedingly cold for some time past, which rendered the condition of those who were but thinly clad very uncomfortable. Every morning they made fires along the road at short intervals. This was a great alleviation to the sufferings of the Cherokee people.

The wooden fort appeared on the horizon. John could see the American flag, and they heard the sound of a bugle. In March 1838 they arrived at Fort Gibson.

The fort was occupied by Lieutenant Colonel Mathew Arbuckle and the 7th United States Infantry. The fort was also the final stop for tens of thousands of Native Americans forced by the U.S. Army to walk the "Trail of Tears" to new homes in Oklahoma. John approached the fort with his long trail of Indians and slaves. Colonel Arbuckle rode out to meet them.

"We have been waiting for you." said the Colonel. "John Ross, I believe."

"Yes, I am John Ross."

"Welcome to Fort Gibson. We thought that you had not made it."

"Have the other Cherokee arrived?" asked John.

"Yes," said Arbuckle, "they have arrived there at the foot of the Ozark mountains, some fifty miles from here." John was so happy to hear this.

"Can you send a scout to tell them we are here."

"It will be a pleasure, Sir. But it looks like your people will need food and water and some rest."

"It's been a long journey." John nodded.

***

By the Ozark Mountains, Oklahoma, a large brass bell was being hoisted up inside a church they were constructing. The Rev. Jesse Bushyhead saw an army scout galloping towards him.

"I have been sent by Colonel Arbuckle at Fort Gibson." The scout called, a little short of breath. "John Ross and the Cherokee have arrived there."

"Well, praise the Lord!" The Rev. Bushyhead lifted his arms.

Five hundred Cherokee and one hundred slaves arrived in the Ozark Mountains of Oklahoma, led by John Ross, Sequoyah, the Rev. Butrick and Doctor Nielsen. Across the horision they could see a thin line of moving figures. Very soon they could see thousands of Cherokees coming towards them. They met in a sunlit valley. Hundreds of men, women and children embraced each other.

"Praise the Lord!" the Rev. Jesse Bushyhead exclaimed. "I thought you would never make it."

"It's been a long journey," confirmed John Ross. "We need food and water, there are many sick and dying."

"Where is Quatie?" asked Jesse.

"She's dead," said John, sadly.

"How?"

"Pneumonia. She died in Little Rock, Arkansas."

"I am sorry, my friend, for your loss." In the distance they saw a group of men ride towards them. Elijah Hicks, Hair Conrad, Daniel Colton, Rev. S. Foreman, Choowalooka, Moses Daniel, James Brown, George Hicks, John Drew, Richard Taylor and Peter Hilderbrand. They dismounted and embraced them.

John Ross wrote into his diary:

"The march ended on March 26, 1839. We were tired and exhausted. The journey had taken five months. Now I had to find out how many had died on this death march that the Indians called the 'Trail of Tears'."

Outside a farm house in the Ozark Mountains, the Indians lay down on the hay. Some were dying, others took food and water from helpful white settlers.

***

In the Baptist church Sequoyah and John talked with the Rev. Bushyhead. Elijah Hicks, Hair Conrad, Daniel Colton, Rev. S. Foreman, Choowalooka, Moses Daniel, James Brown, George Hicks, John Drew, Richard Taylor and Peter Hilderbrand were also in attendance.

"I want to know how many deaths." enquired John Ross.

"Four dead," said Elijah Hicks.

"76 dead." confirmed Hair Conrad. Daniel Colton had counted 204 dead. Jesse Bushyhead had 52 dead. The Rev. S. Foreman announced:

"42 dead." Choowalooka confirmed 180 dead, and Moses Daniel 108. James Brown had counted 142, George Hicks 120 dead. John Drew announced 231, 22 dead. Richard Taylor gave the sum of 85 dead, and Peter Hilderbrand 255 dead. John Ross calculated:

"1,160 dead, Sequoyah, how many were murdred in Tenessee and Georgia?"

"2,014." said Sequoyah.

"How many died on the forced march?"

"Only Elias and John Ridge know this figure." said Sequoyah.

"Do you know where Elias and John Ridge are?" John wanted to know.

"Yes," said Jesse Bushyhead, "about ten miles from here."

John and Sequoyah rode up to Elias Boudinot's house. Elias and his wife Harriet Gold came out on the porch.

"You made it!" Elias seemed pleased to see them.

"Yes, we did. We need to talk." John did not smile. Elias invited them into the house, and Harriet served them some drinks. The inside of the house was cosy. It had not taken them long to set up home and settle in this new place.

"The Cherokee want to appoint me as their leader here." continued John. "What about the Ridge party?"

"The Ridge party exists," said Elias. "I cannot dissolve it."

"It may lead to a war." John warned.

"I know," Elias admitted. "I signed my death warrant, when I signed the treaty. But I believed it was the right thing to do." John noticed how Elias was a little uncomfortable and spoke in the past tense. Does he regret the treaty?

"Where is the money we were promised. It never arrived!"

"I have been informed that it's on its way from Washington." said Elias, but John was not convinced.

"Do you know that your treaty has caused the death of hundreds of people. How many died on the forced march of General Scott's?" Elias took out his list from the desk drawer.

"810," he read. John grabbed hold of Elias's quill and scrawled two figures on

the page.

"3,984 deaths! That is the price of your treaty!" He scribbled 3,984 in large scrawl on the page. Then he threw the quill on the page. No more needed to be said.

***

CHAPTER SEVENTEEN

The Baptist church in the Ozark Mountains is packed with a congregation of Cherokee and slaves. John Ross addressed them:

"I know you have all sacrificed so much to be here tonight. Hundreds have died on this long trek across America." There is silence around the church.

"You will start re-building the Cherokee Nation, like a phoenix you will rise from the ashes. We estimate that four thousand one hundred and five of our people died on this trail of tears. You are the survivors. But don't thank me, thank the thirteen men that led you on this journey. The thirteen men who stand before you will always be remembered gratefully by the Cherokee people. It was these men who led you across two thousand miles of hostile territory. Our deepest thanks go to you. You will always be in the hearts of the Cherokee people. My deepest thanks to Elijah Hicks, Hair Conrad, Daniel Colton, Rev. Bushyhead, Rev. S. Foreman, Choowalooka, Moses Daniel, James Brown, George Hicks, John Drew, Richard Taylor, Peter Hilderbrand and Sequoyah. My deepest thanks also to the many slaves led by Tokpa who helped us on this terrible journey. Without their skill, their bravery and hard work, we would never had made it here. I assure you, as long as you stay on Cherokee land you will be treated as free men until the day comes that the white man abolishes this terrible bond of slavery. I have heard news that in England the Parliament has abolished slavery throughout the British Empire some months ago. I am convinced that it is only a matter of time before it is abolished in America. Finally, my deepest thanks to the Baptist church, who have assisted us on this evacuation of the Cherokee Nation homeland. In re-building the Cherokee nation I ask you to forgive those who signed the Treaty of Encota and not take up arms against them. We have had enough hatred and killing. Now, let's all stand and say a prayer for those who died, and let us pray their memory and also for my dear wife Quatie who sacrificed her life on this terrible journey. It was not only the Cherokee who died on this route west. Today we reached the end of this fateful journey, on March the 26th 1839. Let us try and rebuild our nation of the Cherokee; a great and noble tribe. Let us stand, sing and praise God for our deliverance."

They all stood singing a hymn.

***

An Indian camp was set up and fires lit. A medicine man and some Cherokee were giving thanks to the great spirit while dancing around a fire.

In a tepee six Indians placed six handguns and knives on the ground. They each wrote a number on a piece of paper and threw it in the hat at the table's centre. The older man picked a number from the hat and checked the name. Then he plunged his dagger in front of one of the Indians. The executioner lifted his gun and span the barrel.

At night six Cherokee rode towards John Ridge's house.

At the sound of galloping horses John Ridge got up from his chair and looked nervously at his wife.

"What is it, John?" she asked.

John Ridge stepped out on the porch with a handgun. An Indian jumped up behind him and put a rifle to his head.

"I am here to avenge the four thousand deaths of the Cherokee people. It was you that signed the treaty of Encota without the agreement of the Cherokee nation."

"I felt it was the right thing to do." said Ridge, suppressing his fear. "John Ross

did not send you here." The Indian (name) shook his head:

"I take it upon myself to enact this justice on behalf of the Cherokee people. Because of you and your brother Elias Boudinot, there are thousands of dead Cherokees." The Indian aimed his gun. Ridge's wife rushed out of the house, just as the Indian shot him in the head. He collapsed to the ground. The woman stood wide-eyed with horror. Then another Cherokee turned over the body, checked it and drew a knife and slit his throat. They mounted their horses, turned and escaped. Ridge's wife rushed to his side.

"No, no!" She shouted in disbelief, then knelt down beside his body with tears streaming down her face.

The same group of Cherokee rode to Elias Boudinot's house. Elias was shot dead as soon as he stepped out of his house.

***

Many years later, John Ross recorded in his journal:

"I was deeply saddened by the deaths of Boudinot and Ridge. I did not agree with them, but I never agreed to one Indian killing another. For the way of peace and democracy is the only way. If there is something to be learnt from all this is that killing never served any purpose. After the Cherokees had settled in their new homes and had once again built their government and had begun to prosper, Sequoyah left for Texas and Mexico to find lost Cherokee there."

Sequoyah arrived on horseback at John Ross's new home in Oklahoma. John came out on his porch with his children (and grandchildren?).

"John Ross, my brother," said Sequoyah. "I must say goodbye. I must travel to Mexico to find the lost Cherokee tribe. You have done a great service to my people. You stepped forward when they needed you, you are like the fresh wind blowing over the land. The great spirit will always protect you."

"You could stay, my friend."

"No, I need to find the Cherokee, in Mexico."

"You have done enough for the Cherokee people."

"There is never enough to do for the Cherokee." Sequoyah insisted.

"I will be sorry to see you go." John spoke from the heart. "I fear I will never see you again. It is hundreds of miles across desert country to Mexico."

"The fighting is over." continued Sequoyah. "My work is done here. We Cherokee people are grateful that you led us on this road to peace. It was you, John Ross, who saved these poor people from certain death. Now the Cherokee can look forward to a new future. John Ross, you are one of the rare white men who step forward and help when the Indians and the slaves are in great danger. Why are there not more good men like you? You are like the great spirit protecting my people. God bless you."

"There are many good white men, Sequoyah."

"I am grateful that we met. We have done great work among my people." Sequoyah embraced John and looked him squarely in the face. John sensed that he would never see him again.

"Goodbye my friend." said Sequoyah.

"Before you go, can you give me a name for the new Cherokee capital."

"Call it Tallullah," replied Sequoyah, "after the old Cherokee city in the East.   We must keep the old names." 33.

Nearly thirty years later on April18, 1866 in Washington, John Ross wrote in his diary:

"I never did see Sequoyah again. I learnt later that he and his men suffered hunger, floods, illness and finally death. It is believed that Sequoyah is buried in an un-marked, unknown grave like many thousands of Indians. A man like Sequoyah stands out among the great leaders of the Indian nations, like Gerinimo, Chief Joseph and Sitting Bull. I will never forget his sacrifice. I will also never forget the Cherokee who died on the march west. They were all innocent people.

The estimates of the numbers of Native North Americans at the time of the European arrival in what is now the United States and Canada was ten million. As I write my diary the number of Native Americans had been reduced to 250,000, mainly through imported diseases, dislocation, slavery, mass murder and genocide. In all some 90 thousand Indians were relocated. The Cherokee were among the last to go. Some reluctantly agreed to move. Others were driven from their homes at bayonet point. The Indians now call the route I took and my twelve brave men -The Trail of Tears."

He looked at an old painting of Quatie on the wall. Then he lay down the quill and lifted a necklace with a silver pendant of an eagle. He placed it on a large leather-bound book inscribed with the words 'Cherokee Nation'.

***

Three months later, August 2, 1866 two older grey-haired Baptist ministers, the Rev. Bushyhead and the Rev. Butrick arrived at the Capitol Hotel in Washington. They hurried inside to the reception.

"We have come to claim to body of John Ross, Chief of Cherokee Nation." said the Rev. Bushyhead.

"Rev. Bushyhead, Rev. Butrick." The receptionist told them they had been expecting them.

"We have been expecting you," he said, "thank you for coming, he died during the night. Come with me." The three men walked down the hallway. The receptionist stopped by a door and turned the key in the lock.

They entered the room, where John Ross, aged 78, lay on his bed motionless. In his hands he clasped the necklace that Sequoyah had made for his wife Quatie.

***

EPILOGUE

At the railway station in Washington John Ross's coffin was loaded into a rear carriage. Jesse Bushyhead and Rev. Butrick watched over it. The steam train embarked on a long journey, travelling across the vast landscape of West Virginia, Kentucky, Arkansas to Oklahoma. The train finally arrived on August 9th in Talluquah, Oklahoma. Thousands of Cherokee waited at the train station to see the coffin arrive.

***

In the cemetery of Park Hill, Oklahoma, the coffin of John Ross was lowered into the grave with prayers from the Rev. Bushyhead. A little Cherokee girl threw a beautiful flower on the coffin. The Rev. Bushyhead spoke to a large congregation of mourners:

"We gather here today to remember our Chosen Chief John Ross who dedicated his life to save the Cherokee Nation. The Cherokee People are a proud people. We are a people who have faced adversity and survived. Who have faced trials and adapted? Who have had prosperity and seen it taken away many times over the course of our long history? We are proud to have overcome the many hardships and sorrows with our culture still intact. We come here to remember the greatest Cherokee of our nation, Chief John Ross. We honour his memory."

***

SEAL OF THE CHEROKEE NATION
ᏣᎳᎩᎯ ᎠᏰᎵ
SEPT. 6, 1839